Elkman & McGredy

Look for other Western & Adventure novels by

Eric H. Heisner

Along to Presidio

West to Bravo (I)

Seven Fingers a' Brazos (II)

Above the Llano (III)

Del Rio Hondo (IV)

T. H. Elkman

Mexico Sky

Short Western Tales: Friend of the Devil

Wings of the Pirate

Africa Tusk

Fire Angels

Cicada

Citation for Murder

Flight of the Windigo

Conch Republic, Island Stepping with Hemingway

Conch Republic - vol. 2, Errol Flynn's Treasure

Conch Republic - vol. 3, Coba Libre

Conch Republic - vol. 4, Dominica Dash

Elkman & McGredy

Eric H. Heisner

Illustrations by Al P. Bringas

Visit our website at
www.leandogproductions.com

Amazon: Eric H. Heisner

Illustrations by: Al P. Bringas
Contact: al_bringas@yahoo.com

Cover design: Dreamscape Cover Designs

Author photo by: Dan Farnam

Cover Artwork Source: Thanks to - Carl Bringas Photography

Edited by: Story Perfect Editing Services – Tim Haughian

Paperback ISBN: 978-1-956417-42-5

Dedication

To my screenwriting professors, who taught me how to put my stories on paper.

Special Thanks

Amber Word Heisner, Al P. Bringas,
Dan Farnam & Tim Haughian

Note from Author

One of my favorite stories I put to paper was *T. H. Elkman*. What started as a writing/film project for screenwriting class, turned into an award-winning script that helped fund my independently produced Western TV pilot, *Friend of the Devil*. The story of friendship in the Old West stuck with me over the years and eventually became my second published novel.

Now, ten years later, those characters have reemerged from my imagination to live another wild adventure. I hope the ones who inhabit these stories are like old friends to you. Though it has been many years, we pick up where they left off. Light a campfire, grab a chair, and kick back for another tale on the western frontier.

Eric H. Heisner

October 20, 2025

Chapter 1

Beside a mountain stream, a cowboy squats on his boot heels. After combing his fingers through his months-long growth of beard, he reaches a hand into the running water. Using a metal pan to scoop sand and pebbles from the bottom of the stream, he lets water rush into the bowl and sifts through the contents.

With his wild, grizzled appearance, Tomas H. Elkman looks very much the part of a man left alone in the wilderness. His steady gaze studies the wet mix of gravel in the pan, watching as the water sifts through the layers, letting the heavier particles settle. He touches his hand over the contents, and a faint glint of gold catches his eye. As if a familiar sight, Elkman pinches the tiny nugget from the pan and tucks it into his vest pocket.

Later that afternoon, at another spot along the stream, Elkman uses the same tactics. He sifts gravel through the pan, finds nothing and tosses the contents away. Scooping another, he starts to separate the layers, and then stops when he hears several birds flutter up from the brush behind him.

Without lifting his head or moving to show awareness, his eyes roll upward to scan the immediate surroundings. Apart from water gurgling through rocks, everything is quiet. The hair on his neck prickles, as he senses that someone is watching. His gaze shifts to his rifle lying next to him and then across the water to the bluff opposite.

Suddenly, a gunshot rings out. Elkman drops his pan, grabs his rifle, and hastily rolls away into the nearby bushes. Several more blasts of gunfire explode from the cover of trees. As bullets tear through the leafy branches around him, Elkman, keeping low, crawls through the thick brush. He comes upon an outcropping of rocks and puts his back to it.

The hammer clicks back on Elkman's rifle, and he tucks the gun to his shoulder. He waits for a puff of white smoke, takes aim, and squeezes off a round. He hits the one who fired the shot, and there is a muted yelp from the wounded person. He watches from the rocks, as others scurry from cover to aid their friend. Elkman levers his Winchester and shoots again, skinning a patch of bark from a tree near where they hide.

He levers his rifle, puts another round next to where he hit the first bushwhacker, and waits. The opposing gunfire has ceased, and there are sounds of men dragging someone off. Elkman patiently scans the area through the sights of his rifle, ready to take another shot to defend himself.

Satisfied that his retaliation has put an end to the fight, Elkman lowers his gun, gets to his feet and climbs over the rock formation to take cover on the other side. He waits silently, listening to the wind and watching for movement in the brush. Not hearing anything, he uncocks the hammer of his rifle and lays it across his lap. Eventually, the sounds of birds and woodland creatures return, and the surrounding mountains are peaceful again.

~*~

Carrying his rifle, a bundle of supplies, and the mining pan with a bullet hole in it, Elkman returns to his basecamp. Tucked beneath a tall, rocky overhang, there is a log structure built into the mountainside. Further down, along the cliff wall, is a makeshift corral big enough for his horse and a long-eared pack animal.

Elkman pauses to study the camp for any sign of visitors. Relieved that they haven't yet discovered his cabin, he walks to the dwelling and drops his gear by the doorway. Rifle in hand, he heads to the corral to inspect his stock. The horse comes over. He rubs his hand over the animal's forelock and murmurs, "Well, fellas, it looks like it might be a good time to git gone 'n cash out some of these nuggets."

The animals merely stare at him, as he turns and puts an arm over the top rail of the corral fence. Elkman gazes out at the serene mountain landscape. He reflects on being alone in the wilderness, daunted by the notion of ever being found.

Chapter 2

The sun crests over the mountain and shines on the camp. With a high-cantle saddle strapped on, Elkman's horse stands waiting beside a smaller animal fitted with a wood packsaddle. Elkman comes out from the cabin holding empty pannier bags and slings them over the cross-fork supports of the wooden rig. The animal turns toward Elkman, and the cowboy mutters, "Not much to carry for now... You'll earn yer keep when I buy supplies to bring along."

Elkman secures the load and then looks to his mount. The horse gazes back at him a moment, then lowers its head, shifts to the side, and cocks a leg. Heading back to the cabin, Elkman murmurs as he steps inside. "Just a few more things, and we'll be on our way..."

Crossing the sparsely furnished interior, Elkman goes to a small stove with embers still glowing inside. He touches the tube of metal that snakes its way up and out through the timber roof and then closes the vent on the pipe to shut off the airflow. He scans the primitive dugout, where there are various-sized animal traps, and a few old hides tacked on the wall to keep out of the weather. The rest of the contents in the room consist of a mix of handmade tools and rickety furniture.

Elkman moves past some stools and a small table to a bunk tucked against the back wall. He scoots it away from the chiseled-out cliff wall and then kneels. After a brief glimpse over his shoulder toward the doorway, he rolls a flat slab of stone aside to reveal a cubby carved into the rock.

Reaching inside, Elkman pulls out a cloth tobacco pouch that looks to be filled with sand. After another quick glance over his shoulder, he pulls out another small sack. He rolls the flat stone back, takes the two bags and places them on the table. He moves the bed back to its prior position and does one final scan around the interior of the cabin. Taking the smaller of the two pouches, Elkman tucks it into his interior coat pocket and carries the other one outside to his mount.

~*~

Elkman rides the rugged, high-country of the Oregon Territory with his pack animal in tow, scanning the landscape, watchful for any unexpected encounters. He brings his mount to a halt and slips a finger into his vest pocket to take out tobacco and rolling papers. After rolling the dried leaf, he lights the handmade cig while observing the mountain topography. Trickles of smoke waft through the unkempt moustache that hangs over his mouth. He sits a while, enjoying the solitude, then takes the cigarette from between his lips and smoothes back his whiskers with a thumb. Crumbling the smoldering stub against the palm of his other hand, he tosses it away.

He gives his horse a pat on the neck, and comments, "Yaugh, good to be on the move again." He nudges his spurred heels to the horse's side and trots ahead, encouraging the pack animal to follow by giving its lead line a firm tug.

Chapter 3

Cresting a hill, Elkman rides toward a former military outpost. At the site of the abandoned fort, Samual M. Hindman has filed for a homestead on the land, setting up a store and post office. Elkman rides up to the station, gives it a quick look-over, and then dismounts. He removes his coat, brushes the trail dust off and lays it over the saddle.

After tying his horse to the hitching rail, Elkman looks back at his pack animal. Its lightly loaded panniers shift to the side, as the grazing animal takes up the length of the lead line. Elkman adjusts his hat before fishing out the small cloth pouch from the inner pocket of his coat, and then he heads inside.

Elkman gazes around the store's interior, taking note of the many items for sale. Behind the wood-plank counter, Hindman stands curiously observing the potential customer. Noticing the man, Elkman proceeds toward him, asking, "How's business?"

Hindman grins. "Hopefully *better* t'day with *yers*."

Elkman eases up to the counter and spots a barrel keg with a spigot behind the bar. "Do you have beer?"

"Yessir…!"

"I'll take one."

The proprietor turns and grabs a stout glass mug. Looking over his shoulder as he pours, he studies the bearded westerner standing at his counter. "Where ya comin' from?"

Elkman tilts his head toward the doorway. "Yonder…"

Hindman fills the mug and cuts the foam off the top. "My name is Sam Hindman. Have we met b'fore?"

"Doubt it. First time here…"

Sam turns and places the mug of beer on the counter. "Bin up in the mountains a while, have ya?"

Elkman lifts the mug, and the aroma of the beer hits him. As he drinks, his gaze tilts up to Sam. "Yaugh…"

The proprietor studies Elkman in hopes that he will get more business. Attempting to spark conversation, he asks, "Where ya headed?"

"Camp Polk."

"Yeah…?"

Elkman sets the mug of beer on the counter and smooths a finger under his moustache. He looks out the window to his animals, then nods. "Yep…"

With a smile, Sam places both hands on the counter. "Congratulations. *You* have *arrived*."

After another swig, Elkman swipes away the bit of foam hanging over his lip. "How's that…?"

"How long ya bin up in them mountains?"

"A while…"

"Well, the United States military done pulled up stakes and left this place. I'm homesteadin' this parcel of land now. Runnin' this store and a postal station…"

Taking hold of his mug, Elkman walks to the window and looks out at the remnants of stables and other buildings. He glances over his shoulder and comments, "It's not like the United States military t'jest leave a place."

Sam shrugs. "They stayed here a few years to protect folks from the Indians. Since the Indians ne'er caused problems, they figgered it a waste of time."

Returning to the counter, Elkman leans an elbow on the plank top and gazes around at the store inventory. "I find that if ya don't make any trouble or go lookin' for it, then it usually don't come yer way."

The proprietor nods. "Most of the native folk hereabouts are pretty tame. They ain't as hostile 'n blood thirsty as the ones you'll come upon east of the divide."

"They ain't bin put upon as much."

Sam nods. "Could be… Them big mountain ranges tend to stem the flow of traffic heading west. That culls out the unworthiest of 'em."

As he enjoys his drink, Elkman lets his gaze wander around the building. "This all that's left of the fort?"

"I operate the postal station, if ya'd like to send a letter. Or, if yer 'xpectin' one..."

Thinking back on the time he had mail in Montana, Elkman's eyes momentarily light up with the memory of his old trail partner, Jefferson McGredy. He finds the idea of writing a letter amusing and shakes his head at the notion. "Nope... Don't s'pose I'll be sendin' or 'xpectin' any letters."

Going over to a filing cabinet stuffed with folded papers, Sam turns back to Elkman. "You'd be s'prised what can be found sometimes. The mail goes 'round the world, and some of these letters have bin movin' all over the country fer years. What handle do ya go by?"

Elkman takes another sip from his mug, then grins at the thought of someone sending him correspondence. *"Elkman..."*

Sam scans his gaze over the cubbies and murmurs. "Elkman... E-l-k-m-a-n..." As he thumbs through the papers, he quietly spells it out to himself again. After going through several stacks of postings, he pulls out a folded letter and holds it up with a smile. "Mister *T. H. Elkman...?"*

Chapter 4

With a thud, Elkman sets the beer mug down on the counter and responds. "Yes, sir. That's m'name…"

Sam comes over with the folded paper and smoothes it out on the wooden countertop. "N'er know who's been here..." With a flourishing gesture for effect, he grins and hands it over. "Or, who will come after."

Taking the letter, Elkman examines the name scribbled on the front fold. Dumbfounded, he murmurs, "Who'd mail me a letter… And, how'd they know I'd come through here?"

The proprietor leans over the counter and points to the lack of postmark. "That one wasn't sent from anywhere. Someone paid to leave that note if'n ya happen t'pass by."

Elkman opens the letter, scans the message and then folds it over before tucking it into his vest pocket. Sam stares at the patron's unkempt, grizzled features, and he politely offers, "Ya need me to read it for ya?"

"No, sir... I've learned my letters."

Disappointed at not being able to know the matter of the correspondence, Sam then notices the small pouch that is partly concealed in Elkman's other hand. "Good news, I hope... Anything else I can help ya with? Supplies perhaps...?"

Elkman shrugs while studying items behind the bar. Noticing the proprietor's attention on his cloth pouch, Elkman carefully opens the bag to display the contents on the counter. "Found a few flakes and nuggets up in them mountains."

As he looks to the gold that spills out, Sam's expression shows excitement. "Yes, you did! You bin up there long?"

"Long 'nough..."

Gesturing to the sack, Sam tilts his head at the scale. "Mister Elkman, may I...?"

Elkman nods his approval, and the proprietor takes the sack over to be weighed. He empties the small pieces of gold into the pan with a *tink* and the finer gold-flour pours out after. Hindman gets a register book out from under the counter, opens it, flips over a few pages and finds the table of values. After a brief study of the numbers, Sam turns to Elkman who watches him keenly. "Found all this up in them mountains?"

"Thereabouts..."

"You have mor'n a few dollars here."

"Can you exchange it?"

Sam pencils in some numbers and turns the open book toward Elkman. "When the military fort was still here, they had a quartermaster who could handle such trade. I can give you some in cash and the rest in store credit."

"What if I was to have more of it?"

"How much more?"

Elkman gestures to the scale. "That much 'nd again..."

"I'm afraid, that would deplete all my funds on hand, but I could offer store credit for it."

Movement outside the window catches Elkman's eye, and he turns to see three trail-hardened riders approaching, with a fourth mount carrying an empty saddle. "Let's jest settle up with what I've got there."

With a nod, Sam eagerly empties the gold from the pan into a glass jar and then makes a note of sale in the store journal. Elkman takes out a slip of paper from his vest pocket and slides it across the counter. "Them's my needs..."

Surprised, Sam looks from Elkman's gruff appearance to the scribbles on the paper. "You can read *and* write?"

"I can git by... Fill that order best ya can with what you've got on hand."

Sam tucks the glass jar under the counter and comes up with a lockbox. He opens it, counts out a handful of bills and coins and then slides them over to Elkman. "I'll gather your items and have it ready fer ya shortly. If you'd like a bite to eat, I can have the cook put somethin' together."

"I could stand a good meal." Elkman watches out the front window, as three riders, stopping to inspect his animals, let their gazes linger on his coat and rifle.

Leaning over the counter to see what Elkman is looking at, Hindman offers, "Have a seat at a table back yonder, and I'll bring out what we have on the spit today. Another beer fer ya?"

Elkman lifts his half-finished beer from the counter and starts toward the back of the room, where a few mismatched tables and chairs sit empty. He holds his mug up and replies, "Bring me another with my meal." As the front door opens and the three unknown riders step inside, Elkman observes from the cover of a shelf filled with goods.

Chapter 5

Taking a seat, Elkman keeps his back to the wall, positioning himself to have a good view of the front entryway and counter. The strangers greet the proprietor without noticing Elkman observing from the back of the room. After a brief conversation, they go over to a saddle tack display.

Elkman watches but can't hear the details of what is said. He relaxes back in his chair and finishes the remainder of his beer, as the three men go back outside. Leaning forward to peek out the window, Elkman can see his animals still tied at the rail, unbothered by the curious strangers.

Shortly, Sam comes out from the back room with a plate of food and another mug of beer. "Here ya go...

We have some fresh beef on the rack and all the fixin's." He sets down the heaping plate along with the drink.

Elkman nods his thanks and glances to the door where the strangers departed. "No business today with them fellas?"

Sam glances over his shoulder toward the front of the store and shakes his head. "They said they was aimin' to meet someone and stopped by to see if he'd come by."

"Get many travelers through here?"

"Coach stops to change horses and rest passengers."

"How often a stagecoach pass through here?"

"Once a week... That's the only real commerce that keeps me in business. Folks like you, or the occasional settler comin' in, are few and far between."

"They been through yet?"

"Nope... Due today, anytime..."

Elkman glimpses out the window to see the group of men gathered near the horses at the hitching rail. Sam notices him divert his attention from his meal and asks, "Anything else I can git for ya?"

He turns back to Hindman. "This'll do, thanks."

The proprietor stretches his back straight and wipes his open palms on the front of his vest. "Okay, I'll get yer supplies together and have them ready for you in a bit."

Elkman cuts off a bite of meat and looks up at Sam. "When you have it all together, bring both my animals around the back like you were to stable them." Elkman stabs the meat with his fork, puts it in his mouth, and chews as he continues, "Keep 'em saddled, 'n I'll pack the supplies myself."

Witnessing the rough, bearded customer eat his dinner, Sam nods courteously. "Sure, I can do that. Anythin' else?"

Elkman cuts another bite of meat and continues to chew. "No, sir..."

~*~

Hindman steps outside the store, nods to the men who are now lounging on the porch and heads for Elkman's animals. After untying the horse, he takes the pack mule's lead line and walks them both around to the corrals behind the storeroom. The three strangers briefly pause their conversation, and watch with interest as the animals are led away.

After Elkman finishes the meal, he leans back his chair, rolls a smoke and lights it. With occasional glances out the window, he catches glimpses of the men gathered on the porch. He sits quietly, as the afternoon sunlight catches the lingering haze of smoke. Sam comes from the kitchen and points outside. "The stagecoach is comin' now."

Elkman leans to the side of his chair to peer out another window and spots the stagecoach coming down the roadway. Picking up the empty plate and mug from the table, Sam smiles as the unhurried customer lets out another puff of smoke. "Anythin' else I can git for ya?"

"Nope."

"Yer animals and supplies are all set up for ya out back by the stables. I put in a little extry dried meat to finish out what was left on yer tab."

Elkman drops his chair back onto all four legs, stands, and grabs his hat off a hook on the wall. "Much obliged." Gesturing to the stagecoach coming down the road, he asks, "Git many passengers through here?"

Sam leans down on the table and looks outside at the six-up coach. "Sometimes..."

"Whereabouts do they come from?"

"O'er the mountains to the east, usually headin' to settlements on the coast..."

"Which place is most popular?"

With his hand holding the plate, Sam gestures outside. "Travel to the sunset, and you'll cross the Willamette River. Follow it north a spell to Oregon City, or south to Eugene. You'll find more folks than ya can stand thereabouts."

Elkman mutters to himself. "I can imagine..."

Chapter 6

As the stagecoach comes rattling up to Hindman's Store, Elkman loads his supplies into the panniers of his pack saddle. He listens to the out-front activity of the horses being unhooked from the coach and the unloading of mercantile goods. Not yet hearing anything from the men about waiting on a passenger, he keeps vigilant watch for any unexpected company.

Finished packing, Elkman toes his boot into the stirrup, swings up onto the saddle, and holds the pack mule's lead. Urging his horse on, he trots away from the back of the store, as the team of horses from the stagecoach are led to the corral in exchange for fresh animals. Watching as the rider departs, Hindman offers a wave.

Once a good distance from the outpost, Elkman glances over his shoulder to the three men standing by their horses, talking to a fourth. A chill runs up his spine, as he sees them take notice of his departure and make a gesture in his direction. With a comfortable lead on them, Elkman nudges his horse, bringing both animals to a lope.

As evening sets in, Elkman halts his mount and perks his ear toward his backtrail. Not sensing anything unusual, he breathes a sigh of relief and looks to the last rays of sunshine coming over the mountains. He pats the neck of his horse. "They ain't followin' us, it seems... Prob'ly jest my mind playin' tricks on me as punishment for bein' alone too long." He glances over his shoulder once more to be sure and then, instead of making camp for the night, continues to ride on.

~*~

In the predawn hour, Elkman wakes to a cold campsite. The glow of the sun peeks above the horizon and a morning fog makes it difficult to see very far. Rolling from his blanket, Elkman sits up and looks over at his hobbled animals nearby. As he listens to the chirping of birds announcing a new day, everything stops suddenly.

From his position on the ground, Elkman observes riders emerge from the thick fog and pass a dozen yards away. They appear to be following him from the day prior. He waits, silently watching, as they gradually fade back into the fog.

After rolling his blanket, he quietly lifts his saddle from the ground and carries it to his horse. While he breaks camp, he mutters under his breath. "Huh...

Thought myself as crazy for circlin' back on my own trail like someone on the lam."

As the sun rises and the fog burns off, Elkman leads his animals on foot, moving quietly with his rifle held ready. Cutting his trail where he had decided to double back on his tracks the night previous, he looks down to the valley below. Three men sit horseback, while a fourth dismounts to examine the ground. They converse, as Elkman watches from a distance.

Finally, the tracker follows the trail a few paces, stops, and then scans the whole area before returning to the group. He points. Elkman ducks, as the group looks in his direction.

Tucking his rifle to his chest, he waits. One of the horses below whinnies, and Elkman curses softly to himself when his own animal returns the call. When he peeks over at them again, he sees that the tracker has remounted and is leading the others directly toward him. "Ahh, *damn...*"

Elkman lifts his Winchester, takes careful aim at the lead rider and waits to see if they have discovered his whereabouts. As they ride closer, Elkman suddenly gets the unsettling realization that he recognizes one of them. "No... It *can't be.*" The hair at the nape of his neck prickles, and Elkman lowers his aim to a fallen tree in their path. Just as the foremost rider starts to step over the log, he fires.

The .44-40 caliber slug sends splinters in all directions, putting the four mounts into a panic. The rider in the lead holds tight, as his horse arcs its back and does a crow-hopping dance. After several humping leaps, it finally sends the man flying. Elkman levers his rifle, shooting several more times.

The horses are put to fits of bucking and run wildly off through the woods. Wafts of spent black-powder smoke fill Elkman's nostrils, as he levers the Winchester rifle one last time. He takes aim, waits a moment, and then squeezes the trigger. The last remaining rider tumbles from horseback and clutches his boot where the stirrup had broken free.

Elkman sits up and looks down on the havoc he created. "That should teach 'em t'follow *me...*" Reloading his rifle, Elkman scoots back from cover and heads for to his animals. He gives a reprimanding glare, as he unties their lead lines from a tree and mounts-up to leave. "Don't appreciate ya tellin' 'em where we are." With one last look back, Elkman spurs his horse and tugs the mule along.

Chapter 7

At the place where the trail meets the Willamette River, Elkman stops to decide which direction to go. He looks north, then south, and finally takes out his tobacco pouch and rolling papers to make a smoke. With the rollup dangling from his lip, he makes a quick glance behind to be sure no one is following. Satisfied, he takes a matchstick from his vest, lifts a leg over the saddle horn and strikes the tip across his heel. The match flares, and he touches it to the end of the cigarette.

Gazing out over the slow-moving river, Elkman takes a moment to reflect as he breathes in the tobacco smoke's aroma. He slides the folded letter from his pocket, reads it over again, and then slips it back into his vest. Exhaling a puff of smoke, Elkman tosses the cigarette away and brings his leg back over to fork the saddle. He slips the toe of his boot into the stirrup, looks right, then left, and once again back over his shoulder. Finally, he turns north and rides toward Oregon City.

~*~

His pack mule in tow, Elkman rides down the bustling street of the boomtown. His gaze drifts across the numerous storefronts and then to the diverse crowd filling the boardwalk. As the sea of unfamiliar faces go about their daily business, they pay no heed to his presence.

At the far end of town, Elkman stops at the livery, dismounts, and then lifts the flap of one of his saddle pouches. He pulls out his other gold sack and slips it into his coat pocket. Giving the horse a pat on the neck, he whispers to the animal, "Some business t'take care of, and we'll be clear of this place…"

A stable boy coming out of the barn greets Elkman. "Hello there. Ya need me t'care fer yer animals?"

From his vest, Elkman takes out one of Hindman's coins. "Jest fer a day or so."

"I'll untack 'em, feed 'em, and anythin' else ya need."

The boy eagerly takes the money, and Elkman hands over the reins and lead line to his animals. "That'll do, Thanks" He watches the boy escort the horse and mule into the barn and then turns to face the bustling western town. He takes a deep breath, scratches his neck under his long whiskers and mutters, "Bin a long time since I come to a town. Should prob'ly get bathed 'n barbered-up... After a drink."

~*~

Inside one of the saloons, Elkman, having a glass of beer, stands with his foot on the bar rail. With his back to the room, he keeps his eyes on the open doorway by way of the mirror behind the bartender. Feeling a sense of déjà vu, Elkman hears someone call to him from one of the tables. "Hey there, cowboy! How 'bout joinin' for a hand of draw poker?"

Elkman lifts his mug and turns to look at the card table. His gaze passes over each player, until it lands on the dealer. The gambler's face is unfamiliar, but the motion of shuffling and the gesture to the available chair brings back memories.

Elkman steps over to the table and stands behind the empty chair. The dealer gives a cordial smile and offers again. "Have a seat 'n join us for a friendly game." Elkman takes note that most of the money on the table is stacked in front of the professional gambler. He smoothes his hand over the fresh wad of bills in his vest and can't help but pull back the chair to sit.

"Don't mind if I do."

While curiously eyeing the scruffy, unkempt features of the newest cardplayer, the gambler starts to lay out a hand. "From the looks of it, ya just come in off the range?"

Elkman takes out the paper bills he got from Hindman and notices the skill of the dealer passing the cards around. "Yaugh, bin travelin' through the mountains some."

As the gambler finishes the deal, his eyes twinkle at the sight of Elkman's cash. Tossing a coin to the middle of the table, he smiles gamely at Elkman. "Nice t'have a fresh face in town." He nods to the rest of the players. "Time t'ante-up."

The men toss their money in, and Elkman does the same. He casually looks around at the other cardplayers, and then his gaze returns to the dealer. When the gambler meets his gaze, Elkman asks, "Ya work the tables 'round these parts much?"

"I've been in and out of most houses worth playing. From San Francisco to Portland…"

Elkman peeks at his cards and thinks for a moment. Finally, his gaze drifts back to the gambler and he asks plainly, "Ya ever play 'cross the table with a feller named McGredy?"

Keeping an eye on his hand, the gambler tilts his chin. "Cain't say that I have." He puts his cards face down on the table and picks up the deck. Scanning the men around the table, he grins. "Who's to get this off to an interestin' start?"

Chapter 8

The saloon is now filled with a diverse crowd from the town, from miners to cowboys, and mercantile folk to muleskinners. The great number of people smoking creates a haze that drifts through the air and catches the light streaming in through the open doors. Still at the poker table, Elkman removes his coat. He drapes it over the back of his chair, and adjusts it when he notices the one heavy pocket dragging on the floor.

Looking at the stack of coins and bills on the table before him, he notices that it is much smaller than when he started. Across the table, the gambler's pile has grown much larger. Once again, the dealer rakes in the winnings and sweeps the cards from the table. As he gazes at the players, he chuckles. "When luck goes *my* way, I *hate* to let it end."

One of the cardplayers pushes his chair back and stands. "That's 'nough fer me… I'm busted."

The gambler tosses the man two bits and smiles at him. "My pleasure. Have a drink on me." Disgruntled, but eager to have that drink, the man catches the coin and steps to the bar.

Elkman places his ante for the next round and watches, as the gambler stacks the cards. Despite some fancy exhibition of deck shuffling before he deals out another game, the gambler appears to be legitimate. Examining the hand dealt to him, Elkman sees a pair of nines to stand behind.

Bets are placed on the table, as the next round is dealt. As the dealer's turn comes around, Elkman sees a card slipped from the bottom of the deck faster than the blink of an eye. Unsure if he really saw what he saw, Elkman clenches his jaw and scratches under his beard. He looks down at his own pile of money, around at the others, and then finally to the gambler's nicely stacked winnings. Calmly, Elkman lowers his cards and states, "You said this was to be a friendly game."

A dusty breeze blows in from outside and the gambler's casual gaze shifts to Elkman. "How do you mean, sir?"

"No need for shifty dealin' in a crowd like this."

With all attention on him, the gambler's stare turns cold. "It will *remain* a friendly game, unless *you* say *different*."

Gazes shift to Elkman, holding onto his cards and returning the stare of the dealer. "Yer last card come from the bottom of the deck, accidental-like." As the dispute escalates, the whole room goes quiet.

"You callin' me a *cheat?*"

"Flip that card ya dealt yerself, and we'll see."

Everyone looks down at the table to the last card dealt. Tensions rise, as the other cardplayers begin to get the sense that they've been shorted. Stone-faced, the gambler considers his options and then finally retorts. "I don't know who you are, but I've *ended* men for calling me *less.*"

Firm in his accusation, Elkman responds. "I jest call 'em the way that I see 'em." He slowly places his cards facedown on the table and then gestures to the card in front of the dealer. "Turn that one over, and, if it's not an ace, I'll apologize."

The gambler looks at the card and then back to Elkman. "I'll do no such thing." His hands leave the deck of cards and start to move toward the table edge.

Elkman notices the gambler's movement and sighs. "Grabbin' for a gun only tells me what I already know."

The player next to the gambler reaches out and flips the card to reveal the ace of spades. In a flash, the gambler swings his fist and knocks the man from his chair. With his other hand, he grabs the edge of the table and lifts it. As Elkman scoots his chair back, the table rolls forward, and the money and cards tumble over him. A pistol shot smashes through the underside of the table and lodges in the wall over Elkman's shoulder.

Pitching forward, Elkman pushes the table back at the gambler. It skids sideways across the floor and into the man. Another gunshot splinters through the tabletop, and Elkman looks down to see an exit hole mere inches from his midsection. He pops up from behind the table and thrusts his clenched fist into the gambler's jaw, knocking the man backwards.

The table skids sideways, until two of the legs hit a lip in the plank floor and flip it back onto all four. The stunned gambler is laid out on the floor and the momentum lands Elkman on the table. Another shot rips through the righted game table, barely missing Elkman as he rolls off to the side. Crashing to the floor next to the gambler, he recognizes the deadly look in the man's eyes as the hammer of the pistol clicks back once again. Quick to react, Elkman draws his own gun, cocks it and fires before the gambler shoots.

The blast of the final gunshot quiets the crowded room. The crowd stares at Elkman, holding the smoking handgun, and the gambler, lying dead under the table. As Elkman climbs to his feet, several bystanders are on him, taking the gun from his hand and grasping to restrain him. One of them grumbles, "Yer in trouble, pal…"

Elkman struggles to free himself. "Wait…"

The men hold Elkman back as he kicks out, pushing several more of them away. Managing to pull one arm free, Elkman turns to the doorway. He stumbles forward, aiming to get to the livery barn.

Several men upon him, as he attempts to escape outside, Elkman is suddenly clubbed from behind. As he pushes toward the open doorway, the blow to his skull from the handle of his own pistol blurs his vision. "I only shot in self-defense…" Another whack with the gun drops Elkman to his knees and his hat tumbles to the floor. Hanging defenseless in the arms of the restraining crowd, Elkman fights to keep his vision from spinning out of control. Finally, another solid blow knocks him into a black haze of unconsciousness.

Chapter 9

Laid out on a jail cell cot, Elkman wakes to see the last rays of daylight through a small, high-set window. His gaze travels down to a set of iron bars, then into the sheriff's office and, finally, to the other bed positioned across from him.

Not believing what he sees, Elkman blinks several times. Flashing a grin, Jefferson McGredy stares at him and utters, "Hello, Tomas." Elkman's throbbing head overwhelms him, and he rolls over to pass out again.

~*~

Another day of commerce has the streets of Oregon City bustling with activity. Midway down the main thoroughfare, the sheriff's office and jailhouse occupy a cut-stone building. Inside that jail, Elkman rouses and turns to see that McGredy is still sitting on the bunk opposite. Jefferson scratches his beard, as Elkman sits up. "Mornin', pard…"

Still in pain and not yet trusting his eyes, Elkman touches the lump on his head. "Jefferson…? Is that you?"

"Yep."

"What're ya doin' here?"

"Same as you, looks to be."

Elkman turns to gaze through the bars and into the sheriff's office, which appears to be vacant. He takes a moment to gather his wits and then, finally, turns back to McGredy. "There was an incident at a card game, 'n someone got kilt."

"Who was it?"

"The other guy…"

McGredy nods understandingly and remarks, "Huh. Same thing happened to me."

"Misunderstandin's seem to happen to you often."

"This one wasn't my fault."

Elkman squints an eye, doubtful that McGredy is as innocent as he proclaims. Then he explains, "This fella was caught cheatin' at cards, and then tried to shoot me."

"Yep, same as me…"

With the sound of footsteps from the front office, a man wearing a law badge steps around the corner. Looking stern, Sheriff Landers first peers at Elkman and then at McGredy. "Except there were two that got killed in your little incident."

Elkman waits for the lawman to approach the jail cell. "Mine was in self-defense."

The sheriff leans on the bars to give Elkman a careful looking over. "The folks in that saloon say different."

Surprised, Elkman asks, "What did they say?"

"Said you are new in this town, they don't know you, and you killed 'im for taking too much of your money."

"He was caught cheating."

The sheriff shrugs. "The ones that were there say it was you who started the trouble."

Elkman glances at McGredy, who merely nods his head. Knowing he's in a tough spot, he looks back at the sheriff. "What about the others at the table? They'd vouch for me."

The sheriff wraps his fingers around the bars and gives them a firm jolt to display their strength. "Sorry... The only witnesses to the incident are the ones who brought you in."

McGredy coughs, and Elkman turns to stare at him. Then, his old trail partner innocently mutters, "Same as me..."

Tapping his finger on the bars, the sheriff declares, "Listen here, we are a growing town, and we don't put up with that sort of killin' business anymore. The circuit judge should be through midweek, and a hanging will be held after."

In disbelief, Elkman looks at McGredy, who shakes his head and states, "He told me the same."

Returning to the office, the sheriff calls back at them. "Since you two already know each other, maybe we can have your sentencing done on the same day."

His mind spinning, and in too much pain to argue, Elkman glances at McGredy and lies back down on the cot. Closing his eyes, Elkman mutters, "Damn… Being around you, I always figgered it would come to this."

"I had nothing to do with it."

"No…?"

Staring at Elkman, McGredy relaxes against the wall. "Honest, pard… It warn't my fault *this* time."

"Yeah, mine neither…"

Chapter 10

Elkman stares up at the rough-hewn boards of the jail ceiling. The other bed creaks, as McGredy sits up to swing his legs around and face his cell mate. "How're ya doin'?"

Elkman turns his head slightly to look at the gambler. "Sure didn't 'spect to meet with you again in this sort of place." He shifts on the cot to a sitting position and looks away from McGredy to stare out to the office.

McGredy scratches his chin. "Doesn't look good."

With a sour look on his face, Elkman turns back to him. "No McGredy, it don't look good."

The gambler gets defensive and shows his palms. "Hold it now, Tomas. I'm not the reason you're in here."

"What are you doing here anyway?"

"Had a bit of a scuffle, same as you…"

Cradling his sore head, Elkman stares at McGredy. "No… What are you doing in Oregon?"

"Well, me and that gal-friend of mine in Montana came to an understandin', and I figured it was time for me to head west like you done."

"What kinder understanding?"

Bashful, McGredy takes a moment. "Well… The jist of it was that, if I left town, she wouldn't have me run out on a rail."

"Her love gone sour?"

"Ya *could* say that."

"What did ya do?"

McGredy grins. "I left."

With a grimace, Elkman rolls his eyes. "No… What did ya do t'put 'er off?"

"Nothin' out of the ordinary that I didn't *always* do… Guess she finally saw me for who I *am,* and not for what she *wanted* me t'be."

"What did she *want* ya t'be?"

"A prospect for a respectable husband…"

Not being able to hold back a chuckle, Elkman affirms, "It was only a matter of time."

"Yep…"

Giving Elkman's condition a glance, McGredy rubs his own trimmed beard in reference to Elkman's crop of whiskers. "I see, with the looks of ya, ya ain't bin entertainin' womenfolk. What ya been up to these past few months?"

Elkman smooths his beard and then scratches his neck. "I've been keepin' away from most places."

"Why ain't ya cowboyin' somewhere?"

Touching the tender spot at the back of his head again, Elkman shrugs. "Sometimes ya git to the point where ya jest want to do for yerself 'nd not labor for someone else's dream."

"Hell, I don't wanna work at *all.*"

"Laborin' for yerself ain't so much work."

McGredy stands and climbs onto the edge of the bed frame to peek out the high-set window. "In these boomtowns, easy pickin's at the table is more *my* sorta business."

"And look where *that* put ya."

McGredy smiles and glances back. "Have yerself a look in the mirror 'n see where *yer* at."

"It warn't *my* doin'."

"Welcome to the outfit."

The door of the front office opens, and two men step in. After a brief conversation, one of them stays with the deputy, and the sheriff escorts the other to the cells. Elkman and McGredy, watching as the man is brought to them, instantly recognize the visitor, and they stand, staring, as a wave of annoyance washes over them. Jefferson is the first to speak. "Gol-dammit… *You…?*"

Bob Snarel sweeps back his overhanging moustache and smiles his yellow, corn-toothed grin. "Bin a while, boys…"

The sheriff steps back to the office doorway, just out of listening distance, but keeps a close watch on the odd visitor. Elkman glances at the lawman and then looks back to Snarel. "How'd ya git clear? I figured you'd a'bin hanged by now."

With a smirk, Snarel shakes his head, addressing them. "It appears *yous* are headed fer a short rope and a quick drop." McGredy approaches the bars, and Snarel moves back a step. "Easy now, big fella..."

Moving alongside McGredy, Elkman tersely remarks, "Ya here t'see that we're hanged?"

"Quite the contrary..."

McGredy exchanges a confused look with Elkman.

The visitor tilts his head back toward the main office. "Ya see, I informed the sheriff that you're wanted fer crimes o'er in Wyomin' Territory and, since the judge ain't arrived yet, he's considerin' lettin' me take ya both into custody."

Skeptical, Elkman glares at the outlaw on the wrong side of the bars. "Why would *you* come to help *us*?"

Snarel raises an eyebrow while sweeping a strand of long hair back under his hat. "Consider it a stay of execution." He pivots away from the cell and then glances back at them. "You'll be hearin' from me 'gain soon, be sure of it." He heads into the office, and the sheriff, giving them a tentative glare, follows.

Elkman presses himself against the cell bars, trying to hear the conversation transpiring in the front office. Promptly, the door between them is slammed shut. He turns to McGredy, who has a look of shock on his face. "Are ya okay, Jefferson?"

"If I warn't sober, I'd of thought I was *imaginin'* things."

With a sigh, Elkman returns to his bunk. Staring at the closed door of the office, McGredy listens to the murmur of voices on the other side. Finally, he goes to sit on his own bunk. Looking curiously at Elkman, he notes, "Ya don't seem all that surprised t'see our old associate."

Elkman stares at McGredy for a moment. Then, he takes the folded letter from his vest pocket and offers it to him. McGredy takes the paper, opens it and reads:

Snarel escaped hangman.
Swore to kill you and your friend McGredy.
Keep on the lookout. – J. Mitchell

He looks up at Elkman. "When did ya git this?"

"Few days ago..."

McGredy folds the letter again and then hands it back. "The kid's uncle must be lookin' for Snarel."

"Yep... Left me that note at a waystation."

"And, ya came here to warn me?"

Elkman looks at the broken rays of sunlight streaming in through the bars of the jail window, then back to McGredy. "Had *no* idea where I might find ya."

"But, ya came a' lookin' anyway."

"I needed t'shake off some claim-jumpers that were doggin' me through the mountains."

McGredy thinks and then gestures toward the office. "Was it ol' Bob, ya figure?"

Grimly, Elkman responds, "If it was, he's ridin' with a few others that mean business."

"That's jest great..."

Elkman lies on the bed, and McGredy, in deep thought, leans back against the wall, stroking the whiskers on his chin. "Why ya think he wants to git us out of this place?"

Elkman sighs. "I dunno... Revenge can put funny notions in folks' minds."

With a nod, McGredy suggests, "We're safe in this place. Fer now…" Then, he turns toward the sound of men exiting the front office to the street.

Shifting, Elkman angles his head to look at McGredy, then turns away. "Yeah… For now…"

Chapter 11

Outside the livery stable, Bob Snarel and three others lead their horses with two extra mounts following along behind. Elkman's coat is draped across one of the empty saddle seats. Glancing up the street in the direction of the jailhouse building, Snarel flashes his signature, yellow-toothed grin, puts a boot to the stirrup and mounts.

~*~

With two others, the sheriff enters the holding area and unlocks the jail cell door. McGredy sits up and looks at him. "Sheriff, is the judge here already?"

He swings the barred door open and waves them out. "No need for him to be wastin' his time on the likes of *you*."

Elkman looks at the two men directly behind the sheriff. "Is this a lynch-mob ya brought with ya?"

The lawman snorts. "Not yet… Git up, 'n clear out. These fellas are takin' you to stand trial for your other crimes."

Rising to his feet, McGredy peeks around the sheriff to the rugged pair behind him. "*What* other crimes…?"

"The bounty-warrant says multiple horse-thefts and the murder of a young cowboy."

Elkman senses that protesting the warrant will only delay things, so he gets up from the cot and puts on his hat. McGredy grabs his coat to stand alongside him. He glances aside at his former trail partner and grumbles under his breath. "So much for protection under the law…"

The sheriff ushers them both out of the cell, and they march through to the front office. Looking for a way out of this, Elkman eyes the rifle rack and the locked chain securing them. His gaze meets McGredy's and the gambler shakes his head. "The odds ain't with us on this one…" Meeting the cautious stares from the deputies in the room, they proceed outside.

Snarel, horseback, greets Elkman and McGredy, as they step onto the boardwalk. He is cleaned-up, as if he had just come into some money. Tipping his hat to greet the sheriff, Snarel then grins at the pair of prisoners. "Mornin', fellas…"

McGredy stomps his heels in protest and whirls around to face the sheriff. "Well, hell… He's no sort of law!"

The lawman pushes McGredy toward one of the horses with an empty saddle. "He has a warrant for your arrest and will take custody of you both."

Snarel, pleased with himself, sits upright and pushes back in the seat of his saddle. "Come along, Mister McGredy. You can go it easy, or the hard way." Flushed with anger, McGredy steps down from the boardwalk and goes to mount. He notices that it's his own saddle and gear, with his rolled blanket tied on behind the cantle. He looks over at his captors, and Snarel grins. "I rounded up most of yer things. And, I even made sure ya had yer blanket."

McGredy snorts, "I'll thank ya later, you can bet."

Elkman steps off the boardwalk, goes to his own horse, and looks at his coat tied behind the cantle. The pocket that had held his sack of gold is flat and empty. Easing his horse beside Elkman, Snarel whispers, "The findin's in yer pockets were a lot more useful than what I found in that card-peddler's poke." He sweeps back the lapel of his new coat to show off a clean shirt and vest.

Elkman scratches underneath his rough beard and sighs. "Ya spent it on a new outfit?"

His dark eyes twinkling, Snarel replies, "A good bit of it was put to use in helpin' with your release into my custody." The outlaw pulls back his coat at the hip and places his palm on his belt which has Elkman's pistol holstered on it. "Money well spent, wouldn't ya say?"

Elkman lifts his chin and looks out past the town limits to the mountains beyond. "I can think of other ways."

Snarel laughs. "We used a bit of it fer other activities, too. Gotta keep these rascals happy."

When Elkman casually scans his escort, he notices they aren't packing any supplies. "How about my mule?"

With a sweeping gesture down the street, Snarel grins. "We'll pick it up on our way outta town."

"We headed back to Wyoming?"

"You'll find out soon 'nough." Offering a departing wave to the lawmen, Snarel ushers the pair of captives away. He calls out. "Good day, Sheriff... Nice doin' business with ya."

The sheriff steps back, leans on the door frame and hooks a thumb in his belt. "Take 'em away from here. I don't expect to see *any* of you in my county *ever again*"

Riding alongside McGredy, Snarel adjusts his hat. "Seems like ya wore out yer welcome here..."

McGredy grumbles, "The feelin's mutual..."

They ride down the street and then stop in front of the livery barn. The boy brings out Elkman's mule, loaded with supplies, and hands over the lead. Offering a reluctant nod, Elkman takes the rope and looks from the stable boy over to Snarel. "Did ya pay the kid?"

"He's bin paid."

The curious youngster gives the unusual group of riders a look-over. Taking a few steps back to the shelter of the barn, he watches as the men ride out of town.

Chapter 12

The riders head into unsettled territory, with Elkman at the front of the party, his pack mule in tow. Slightly behind him, Snarel keeps a watchful eye, as the others follow with McGredy. After riding silently for a long while, Elkman slows his mount, letting Snarel ride up beside him. He glances aside. "Ne'er said where we're goin'…"

Snarel looks behind at the others, then back to Elkman. "I was a bit late to the gatherin', but the boys said ya had a nice little gold camp up in them mountains."

"It weren't my place to keep. Jest an old dugout cabin where I stayed a while…"

"From what I found in yer pocket, it was successful."

Elkman pushes back his hat to scratch his forehead. Readjusting his lid, he shakes his head. "Not from any diggin'... Jest what I found pannin' the stream."

Snarel peers back at McGredy and then to those beside. "First off, all I could think of was how to get even with ya both. After hearing 'bout yer findin's, I've since had other ideas."

"Ya think we're gonna set up a gold-pannin' operation in the mountains for you?"

"If there's gold nuggets 'n flakes settlin' in them rivers, there's even *more* to be dug outta the ground."

"McGredy and I don't know nothin' 'bout minin'."

Snarel's eyes twinkle with glee. "My new cohorts do, and all they need is a few strong backs to do the diggin'."

Elkman glances behind at McGredy and then the others. "I don't think I'm speakin' out 'a turn, but work ain't to McGredy's likin'. So, you'll *probably* have ta *kill* us."

A grin appears under Snarel's overhanging moustache, and he pushes back his overcoat to put a hand on his firearm. "That's in the cards, as well."

~*~

As evening sets in, Elkman and McGredy sit near a small campfire. Over by the packmule and horses, the others are putting together a meal from the contents of Elkman's pack. McGredy leans over and whispers, "Where they takin' us?"

"Up into the mountains..."

"Why they keepin' us around? Figgered ol' Bob would do away with us first chance he got."

"They want us to dig for gold."

In disbelief, McGredy stares at Elkman. "I ain't a damn gold miner 'n wouldn't know where t'find it."

"They jest need us t'do the diggin'."

With a shake of his head, McGredy leans over and states, "I'd rather *win* it than *dig* fer it."

"Doubt we'll be playin' many cards with this bunch."

"Hell, why don't he jest *kill* us?"

"That's the other plan propos'd, if we don't go along with what he wants."

McGredy stares at the flames of the campfire, digs his heels into the ground and grumbles, "I *knowed* that fella was trouble the first time we laid eyes on 'im."

Approaching the fire, Snarel peers down at the pair. "Reminiscin', or jest schemin' agin me?"

Elkman looks up from the campfire to stare at him. "Mister, we always gave you a fair shake."

"That's why *I'm* givin' ya one."

McGredy attempts to control his anger. "Havin' us dig yer gold claim for ya is a fair shake?"

"What claim...? We ain't got no registered gold claim." Snarel smiles at them. "We'll jest be takin' a bit of what the mountain has to offer. Same as what yer pal Elkman done..."

Surprised, McGredy turns to Elkman. The cowboy merely shrugs and replies, "I was jest passin' through the area and found a few nuggets in the stream."

Looking back at Snarel, McGredy shakes his head. "Carvin' into a mountainside is a whole lot diff'rent than splashin' 'round on a riverbank."

Snarel's eyes flicker in the firelight. "Got ya outta jail, 'n saved ya from the hangman. It's better'n what ya done fer *me.*"

Elkman replies with contempt. "Ya brought that upon yerself, 'n ya got us outta jail with the help of *my* findin's."

The outlaw glances over his shoulder at his partners and lowers his voice as he speaks to Elkman. "They say ya found a good spot that was thought to be picked over years ago. Well, since ya turned up some color, it turns out it warn't."

McGredy folds his arms across his chest and pouts. "Dadgummit, I ain't diggin' ta get *you* rich."

Snarel feigns kindness, as he stares at the two captives. "Who knows, we may find 'nough gold to git us *all* wealthy."

The gambler scowls back. "Not likely…"

"Yer as disagreeable as when first we met!"

"The feelin's mutual…"

Snarel paces in front of the campfire, then finally looks down at them. "While the two of ya conspire to git clear of *me,* them boys are doin' the same on gittin' rid of *you*. So be careful, or ya jest might end up with bullets in yer backs."

With one of his sinister grins, Snarel turns away and steps out of the firelight. One of the other men comes over and tosses them a sack of dried jerky. They look at him, waiting for something more, but he turns and walks off without a word.

Chapter 13

Elkman, leading the group, rides on toward the mountains. They follow the wheel-cut of a coach road that makes its way through the trees, as they gradually move to higher elevations. Snarel rides past Elkman's pack mule and eases up beside him. "How long we gonna follow this road?"

Elkman smoothes his moustache and glances at him. "Seems to be goin' in the right direction 'n should git us across this range. We can come down past Hindman's store."

Snarel grunts. "Jest missed ya there, didn't I?"

Recalling that Snarel was the one on the stagecoach that they were waiting for that day, and who then followed him, Elkman smirks. "Could say, *I* jest missed *you* the next day."

"Yer a smart one, but don't git ta thinkin' yer *too* smart, or I'll end this trip for ya real quick."

Elkman gazes around at the mountains. "I think I can find my way from the old army post back to that minin' camp. Don't think I could locate it wanderin' through high country, comin' from the other direction."

With a flourished wave toward the trail ahead of them, Snarel grins. "Then, lead on, Tomas Elkman..."

~*~

After making their way over the mountain pass, the riders travel south, keeping to the road leading toward Hindman's General Store. Snarel, ready for any chicanery, keeps a close eye on Elkman. Easing his horse alongside again, Snarel points down the road. "That'll be the stagecoach station jest o'er that rise." He points west. "Ya should be able to find yer way jest fine from here."

"Ya still got any of my gold dust?"

Snarel looks at him prudently. "A bit, maybe..."

"Should resupply before headin' in them hills."

"I think we have 'nough with what *you* provided."

"Sure thing... *We* do, but what about them others?" Elkman nods over his shoulder toward the riders behind."

"They'll make do."

"The last few days, they've made do with what was to last me a *month.* Do it now, or we'll hav'ta send someone later."

Snarel considers his options. "Okay... But, if ya try anythin' shifty with that shopkeep, I'll jest end it right there fer the both of ya."

Elkman stares forward at the trail ahead as he rides on. When they crest the rise, below they see the former military compound and Hindman's store. With a cluck to his horse, Elkman urges his mount and the mule in tow.

At the store, Elkman studies a pair of saddled horses tied to the hitching rail. As he starts to dismount, Snarel reaches out and grips Elkman's coat sleeve. "Remember, *friend…* I git any inklin' that yer gonna squeal, I'll burn ya down."

Elkman peers at Snarel's hand on his arm, nods and shakes off the man's grip. He dismounts, ties his animals alongside the others, and then steps up onto the front porch. Snarel pivots in his saddle to address the riders behind them. "We're goin' ta git a few things. You boys keep McGredy here. If he even *looks* crosswise, shoot 'im."

McGredy relaxes back in the saddle and looks at each of the riders beside him. "Why don't one of ya git us some whiskey while we're here?"

Dismounting, Snarel shoots a glare at the gambler. "Maybe I will, but none fer *you…*" After tying his mount to the hitching post, he climbs the steps to the porch and stands next to Elkman. Before they go in, Snarel sweeps back his coat, draws his gun and conceals it behind Elkman. "Now, hurry 'n git what's needed. Don't worry 'bout payin' fer it. *I* got it." Amused by his own joke, Snarel smiles as he nudges Elkman forward and they enter.

Chapter 14

Inside Hindman's store, Elkman and Snarel go to the sales counter to find that no one is tending to it. As they approach, they notice a couple having a meal at the back of the room. Snarel prods Elkman with the barrel of his gun and whispers, "Pay no heed to them. Let's jest git what we come in fer."

Elkman guesses that the horses outside belong to them, but suddenly, has to catch his breath as his heart skips a beat. He takes note of the young woman seated at the table and promptly recognizes Amy Martin. His memory flashes back to their brief encounter at her father's horse ranch in Colorado. Elkman wonders who the other one is but can't make him out. She looks in their direction but, not recognizing either man, goes back to eating her meal.

Self-consciously, Elkman puts his hand to his over-grown beard and rakes his fingers through the long whiskers, realizing why she doesn't acknowledge him. His musings on the past are disturbed by the barrel of a pistol being pressed into his ribcage and Snarel hissing, "What's wrong with you? Ain't ya ever seen a pretty gal b'fore?" Elkman turns away, and Snarel pops the service bell with the palm of his empty hand. With a chuckle, he adds, "Good thing them others ain't in here, or we'd have 'em sniffing that heifer's petticoats."

When Hindman comes out from the back to serve them, he brightens at the sight of the familiar patron. "Back so soon? Town life must not be that agreeable to ya." Then, looking to Snarel and recognizing him as the passenger on the stagecoach, the storekeeper feels a tinge of apprehension. "You two *know* each other?"

Snarel responds, "We're old acquaintances."

After looking down to see that Snarel has something concealed in his hand, Hindman addresses them with a smile. "*T. H. Elkman,* wasn't it? What can I do fer ya this time?"

When the name catches the attention of the two in the back, they stop their meal, and the man pushes his chair back. Snarel takes out the diminished sack of Elkman's gold and plops it on the counter. "We'd like to git a few more supplies."

Looking at the small pouch, Hindman recognizes it and looks up at Snarel suspiciously. "Is that right…?"

Snarel flashes his mischievous grin. "Yaugh, yaugh… We's ol' travelin' pals are needin' some extry things."

The storekeeper slides a pencil with a pad of paper across the counter to Snarel. "Write down what items ya need, 'n I'll git 'em from the stock room."

Snarel realizes that he can't write while still holding the gun, so he nudges Elkman. "You write down what we want." As Hindman watches them curiously, Snarel turns away a bit to conceal that he is holding a weapon.

Elkman flinches from the gun pressed into his spine and leans on the counter to pick up the pencil. At the table in back, the movement is noticed, and they whisper to one another before continuing with their meal. Elkman looks at Hindman. "We'll be needin' more of the same as last time."

Outside the store, McGredy dismounts and squats to stretch his legs. He pats an open palm to his growling midsection, sniffs loudly, and then looks at the other riders. "Ahh, I can smell 'em fixin' up some tasty grub in there."

From horseback, they stare at him. Then, one of them rides over to Elkman's pack saddle and pulls out the bundle of dried jerky from the pannier. With a grin, he tosses it to the ground at McGredy's feet. They laugh, as he looks up at them with disappointment. "Yer a pack of mangy coyotes with no sophisticated palate." He bends to pick up the bundle, takes out a piece of dried meat, and bites off a chunk.

As he chews, the front door of the store creaks open. Elkman steps out and heads down the stairs to the hitching rail. He glances at McGredy chewing the jerky, then checks inside the pannier to take inventory of their other supplies. Behind, Snarel mounts his horse and turns the animal to face the others. "The fella inside is gatherin' things, and we'll be on our way."

McGredy looks up at him. "Whiskey…?"

Without answering the gambler, Snarel merely looks over at Elkman. "*Git away from there.* I don't want ya havin' words with anyone. One of *us* can pack them things."

In compliance, Elkman goes to his horse, unties it from the hitching rail and steps beside to mount. As his leg swings over the saddle, the front door to the store opens again and Hindman comes out with two flour sacks filled with supplies. The storekeeper moves to the top of the stairs and then stops. From the shadows behind him, two figures emerge, one of them holding a rifle.

Turning his horse, Snarel eyes Hindman suspiciously, then notices the two standing behind him at the doorway. "Bring them supplies o'er here…" He gestures to one of his riders to go and get the sacks from storekeeper.

Hindman sets both bags down at the edge of the porch. "I'd like to speak with Mister Elkman a moment."

Snarel grumbles back. "No… We gots to git movin'…" Seeing the gambler standing next to his horse, Snarel growls, "Mount up, McGredy…"

Quietly observing, Elkman sees Amy and her uncle, James Mitchell, slowly step behind Hindman. She stares at him, still not quite able to believe that it is really him under the month's growth of unkempt whiskers.

Snarel moves his horse away and places his hand on the grip of his holstered revolver. He whispers harshly to Elkman. "Follow me, or I'll shoot ya right here in front of these folks."

Reins gathered between his fingers, Elkman turns his horse to follow. From the shadows of the porch behind them, he can hear someone stepping forward on the boardwalk, and then a female's voice calling out. *"Tomas H. Elkman…?!"*

Chapter 15

Stopping his mount, Elkman turns in the saddle to look back. His heart feels like it will pound through his vest, as he stares at the young woman standing in the sunlight on the porch. Wanting to call out to her, he can't seem to find the right words. From the corner of his eye, he spots Snarel drawing his gun.

Aware of what is about to happen, Elkman spurs his horse straight into Snarel's mount and leaps from horseback to tackle the man from his saddle. As they tumble to the ground, Snarel shoots his pistol, and the bullet goes astray, smashing into the Hindman's Mercantile Store sign above the doorway. The gunfire startles the horses, and the riders grab their guns.

On the ground, McGredy rushes for the nearest man, drags him from horseback and smashes a fist into his face. "That ought to teach ya to sass me with a sack'a jerked beef!" After he tosses him aside, he goes after the next. Instead, a shot from the rider's pistol kicks up dirt near the gambler's feet, and McGredy dives under a riderless horse to use it as a shield.

On the porch, Hindman kicks the sacks of supplies aside and rushes to find cover behind an overturned whiskey barrel. James Mitchell aims his rifle and shoots one of the riders. Merely wounded, the man keeps to the saddle, while James levers his Winchester to take a shot at the other one.

Both remaining riders have their guns out, and one of them shoots at McGredy. The other one aims toward the store. He fires a round which shatters the side of a porch-post near Amy, and she ducks aside as splinters rake across her face. Seeing blood on her cheek, her uncle hollers while levering another round into the chamber. "You hit, girl? Git *down!*"

James Mitchell aims, but before he can pull the trigger, one of the riders fires a shot, striking him in the pelvis. The shot takes his legs out from under him and, as he falls to the porch, he drops his rifle. Amy grabs it, just as another round skitters off the wooden deck.

In the midst of it, Elkman and Snarel exchange blows, wrestling one another like a pair of angry mountain lions, smashing their fists into each other and grappling to get the upper hand. The nearby horses jump clear of their path.

McGredy notices the man he had just pummelled get up and start to pull his pistol. Slipping around the horse he was using for cover, he charges the dazed man and tackles him to the ground. Grabbing the gun away, McGredy swings it hard across the man's face, putting him out of the fight again.

Amy fires at the wounded rider with her uncle's rifle, knocking him out of the saddle. She levers the Winchester, hurries a shot at the last man still mounted, and misses. Levering another round into the chamber, she takes steady aim, as the outlaw turns to point his handgun at her. He clicks on an empty chamber, assesses the hopeless situation, and turns his horse to flee. Amy takes the shot, merely grazing the man's flapping coattail as he gallops away.

The shooting ceases and the fistfight comes to an end, as Elkman and Snarel stand to catch their breath. They look at a loose gun at their feet and then to the outcome of the skirmish. One of the riders lays sprawled-out, dead, while the other slumps near McGredy's horse, cradling a bloody head wound. On the porch, Amy levers the action on the rifle, as her uncle leans against a support post, clutching his injured hip.

In utter exhaustion, Elkman and Snarel exchange looks of defeat and lower their clenched fists. Straightening up, Elkman sighs heavily, then leans down to grab his hat from the ground and then reshape its crumpled form. "I think we're done here…"

Snarel looks around, spits a mouthful of blood and glances once more at the dropped pistol. "Not hardly…"

From the porch, Amy yells as she lifts the aim of the rifle. "Are you the fella named Bob Snarel?"

He turns and stares at her a moment, then flashes a grin. "Yaugh… The one and only…"

Her finger wraps around the trigger, and she lines-up the Winchester's sights directly on his chest. As everyone waits to see if she will shoot, she adds, "You killed my brother!"

The arrogant grin fades from his features. "Could be… I've killed lots of folks." He takes a step toward her and opens his coat to show that he is unarmed. "I ain't got a gun on me. Now, ya gonna shoot or not, little lady?"

Amy stares down the rifle barrel at him, takes a breath, and then finally lowers her aim. "I'll see you hanged, instead."

With a hint of the grin still lingering, Snarel replies, "Missy, I've heard them same 'xact words spoke at me b'fore, 'nd it ain't happened yet."

Realizing that Amy doesn't have the stomach to murder a man in cold blood, McGredy marches over to Snarel and swings the butt of his pistol across the back of the man's skull. The outlaw crumples into a heap on the ground, as McGredy stands over him. "I've heard 'nough of his damn talk…"

With a nod of approval, Elkman grabs his pistol from the ground and spins the cylinder to check the remaining rounds. Both men turn to look at Amy on the porch, and Elkman utters, "It's good to see ya again, Miss Martin."

"Tomas… You better call me *Amy*."

McGredy grunts. "When the gal is holdin' a durn rifle, ya best call 'er whatever she likes."

Elkman tucks his gun in his waistband, looks around, and then answers her. "Nice to see ya… Amy…"

Chapter 16

Slumped against the wall of Hindman's store, Snarel wakes to find his hands tied. On the floor next to him is one of his associates sporting a blood-soaked bandage around his head. Across the way, the storekeeper has his doctoring supplies out and is tending to the bloody wound on James Mitchell's thigh. James winces from the pain, as he drinks from a whiskey bottle.

After Hindman finishes bandaging, he wipes his hands. "The bullet passed through, but it hit part of the pelvic bone." He stands to address them. "Not sure if the bone is broken or just grazed, but you shouldn't move the leg before it's healed."

James lowers the bottle and looks at him. "How long…?"

"Could be a month, maybe more…"

James takes another swig from the bottle, and then he glances at Snarel and the other rider. "What about those two?"

Hindman turns to look at them and shakes his head. "The one with the head injury shouldn't travel either."

Elkman pushes his chair back, stands from the table where he was sitting with McGredy, and then addresses Hindman. "What d'ya propose we do?"

"Sorry, I can't let ya stay here. But, I can loan ya a wagon and team to get ya somewhere's else."

Finished with a plate of food, McGredy wipes his mouth. "Why cain't we stay here?"

Hindman turns to him. "There's a *dead man…*"

McGredy grins. "He won't be causin' us any trouble."

The storekeeper wrings his hands. "The one that rode away surely will. What happens when he brings others?"

James takes another pull from the bottle, glares at Snarel, and then grumbles, "We have warrant papers on that one there. Let's hang 'im now and save us taking 'im back to Wyomin'."

Hindman stands firm. "I will not tolerate a lynching! Your business is much appreciated, but you'll need to find someplace else to hold up and keep those men."

Glancing outside, Elkman studies the dirt roadway. "When is the next stagecoach due?"

Hindman shakes his head. "Not till next week…"

McGredy pushes his plate aside and sits up in his chair. "If that feller rides to Oregon City, he could round up folks to join him in comin' back."

Elkman nods. "And that's jest a few days away…"

McGredy adds, "They might even take the stagecoach."

Standing in the corner, Amy clears her throat and addresses everyone. "We are going to take that man to Wyoming to hang for his crimes. I can purchase the wagon for my uncle, and we will head out on the morrow."

McGredy gazes at her. "What about the posse that will most likely be comin' after us? With us totin' a wagon, they'll be able t'follow and catch us right quick."

"We will make our way and hope for the best."

Elkman paces across the room and then turns to them. "I'm not gonna risk bein' taken by a hostile mob and then stand before a judge for what happened at a card game."

Amy stares at him. "We can't leave my uncle behind, and I will *not* let that man escape punishment *again.*"

McGredy senses his old trail partner is forming a plan. "What're ya thinkin', Tomas?"

"We keep to where we were originally headed."

"Yer gold camp in the mountains…?"

Elkman nods. "It's not far. It's hard for others to find, and I think we could hole-up there a good while."

Skeptical, McGredy notices that Snarel seems to perk up at the idea. "What about *him*?"

"We bring them both along and keep an eye on 'em, until things settle and we can safely travel back to Wyoming."

James pushes up against the wall, takes another drink and cradles the whiskey bottle in his lap. "I should be able to travel in a few days."

Elkman looks toward Hindman, who shakes his head. After a moment, Amy, worried, asks, "If anyone comes after us, won't they follow our wagon tracks into the mountains?"

Elkman answers. "Where we're goin', off the beat'n trail, we won't be able to take a wagon."

McGredy adds, "When I was scoutin' fer the gover'mnt, I tracked Indians that used travois in places ya can't imagine."

Amy looks to her uncle with concern and then glances at the bandaged man sitting next to Snarel. Hesitantly, she offers, "We'll make two and carry the wounded that way."

After nudging his wounded associate, Snarel pipes in. "Jest one'll do…" Everyone looks, as he gestures to the collapsed man next to him. "No use carryin' dead weight."

Chapter 17

An axe blade swings and sinks deep into the trunk of a tree. Elkman pulls back the handle, heaves it over his shoulder and makes the last cut before watching the tree fall. He turns to McGredy nearby and comments, "Since I done the choppin', you can strip the limbs and trim it off at a dozen or so feet."

McGredy picks up a hatchet and starts to hack off the branches on the long, straight pole. "Ya know, it seems like whenever I'm around you, I get myself into a job o'work."

"Or trouble…"

McGredy smiles, as he whacks at the smaller limbs. "What d'ya think 'bout that gal from Colorado comin' all the way out here to warn ya?"

After selecting another similar-sized tree, Elkman starts to chop at its base. "She didn't come here for me."

"Is that what ya think?"

"She come to avenge he who kilt her brother."

McGredy stops cutting and stands to look at Elkman. "Her brother is dead."

"So…?"

"She's here to give warnin' fer *you*, not fer *him*. If it was jest to git revenge, the uncle could have done it 'nstead."

Elkman rests briefly on the axe handle and scratches under his beard. "I only got to know her a day or so."

McGredy laughs. "I guess ya got to know 'er a lot better'n I did durin' our short visit."

"Not by much…"

"When a gal gits it in her craw that she wants somethin', neither hell nor high water will stop 'er from gettin' it."

Elkman lifts the axe and inspects the blade's sharpness. "Then, she's jest wastin' her time. I ain't the settlin' down type."

"Not yet, ya ain't…"

Elkman swings and buries the blade in the trunk. "Why didn't ya stay at the store instead of botherin' me?"

"The temptation ta kill that fella was too great fer me. I'm hopin' they git the job done while we're gone."

"They ain't them kind of folks…"

McGredy goes back to whacking away at the branches. "That uncle of hers was just one more slug of whiskey away from jerkin' his hog leg and slappin' a load of lead into him. Did ya notice how Bob got awful quiet?"

Wood chips fly, as Elkman swings another blow into the tree. "Would be a lot simpler for us if he had."

"Things woulda bin a whole lot simpler if'n we woulda taken care of him back when we had the chance, instead of gettin' the help of that Territorial Marshal."

"I don't go agin the law."

"What 'bout bustin' jail?"

Elkman continues to chop. "I was ready to stand trial."

"And hang fer it...?"

With one more hard chop, the tree starts to topple over. "Doesn't matter any now."

McGredy stops his work to witness the timber falling. "Ya ne'er know if Lady Luck is gonna deal ya a decent hand or jest a dead man's draw of aces 'n eights ta play."

They watch the tree hit the ground and come to rest. Then, Elkman starts cutting the trunk clean of its branches. "Luck has got nothin' to do with it."

~*~

Elkman and McGredy ride from the wooded area leading the pack animal fastened with the makeshift litter slung between two long poles. After arriving at Hindman's store, they wait in front, as Amy comes outside with sacks of supplies. She turns to watch as Hindman and Snarel carry her uncle on a stretcher made from a blanket.

The wounded man winces at the awkward carry. "Durnit…! Let me try to walk. This hurts more'n bein' shot."

As they cross the porch, Snarel smiles and purposefully bangs the sling into a support post. Amy's uncle howls with pain, and Hindman glances back. "Watch it there, fella!"

Making little effort to be careful, Snarel raises his end of the improvised stretcher, and they make their way down the steps to the waiting horses. He grumbles under his breath. "Hell, I'm doin' what I can fer 'im that wants me strung up."

James shifts to ease the pain, and then glares back at him. "If I had my pistol with me, I'd shoot ya right now!"

When they reach the horses, Snarel gladly drops his end. Groaning with discomfort, the wounded man gives him a cold stare and attempts to roll over into the travois. While Hindman helps James try to get comfortable, Amy brings over the sacks of supplies to tuck around her uncle.

When Elkman dismounts, Amy goes to him. "Now that the whiskey's worn off, he's in a lot of pain."

"I reckon that would put anyone in a sour mood." Elkman inspects the supplies tucked around James and sees that the constant pain has turned the man's complexion pale. "Sir… Can I git ya anythin' b'fore we start on our way?"

The old rancher clenches his jaw, heaves a heavy sigh and looks up at Elkman. "Another bottle of that medicinal whiskey would make me feel some better."

Elkman turns to look at Amy who shakes her head. "Hold on... I'll see what I can do for ya." He finishes securing the load on the travois and glances over at McGredy who sits watching from horseback. He receives a grim expression from the gambler and then walks back to have a word with Amy. "Yer uncle is gonna need somethin' more for the pain."

Standing nearby, Hindman lowers his voice to them. "When he drinks too much of the pain away, he gits the idea he can git up and walk if he wants." Hindman glances over at the patient and then ushers Elkman and Amy another step away. "Need to keep him sober 'nough to where he won't use that leg, or the bone won't set and it'll never heal proper."

Amy watches her uncle shift uncomfortably on the travois and then turns to Elkman. "I know he's in terrible pain, but if he gets too liquored-up, he gets hard to handle."

As Elkman ponders the setup, he watches her uncle continue to squirm with discomfort. "It's gonna get a whole lot worse when we get to draggin' 'im along the trail."

Amy sighs, "Should I give him what he wants?"

"Save the bottle for when we are jest 'bout to leave here. He'll need somethin'... We can strap 'im down, if need be."

As Amy nods with understanding, Hindman turns to see Snarel slowly making his way toward Elkman's horse. "Mister, ya better watch that one."

Elkman turns to observe Snarel casually leaning on the hindquarters of his mount. "McGredy… Keep an eye on him. I'm gonna git the other horses saddled."

With a nod, McGredy pushes back from the saddle horn and straightens up in the seat, pulling his broad shoulders back. "I was jest waitin' fer that rascal to slip a boot in yer stirrup." He grins. "That way, I could plug 'im with good cause."

Over the hindquarters of the horse, Snarel peeks toward McGredy and pats the animal on the rump. "I was jest checkin' t'see that the cinch warn't too tight."

McGredy waves a hand. "Be my guest and check away. I'm more'n eager to be done with ya."

Elkman shifts his attention from McGredy to Amy. "Tend yer uncle best ya can, 'n keep yer distance from that 'un." She looks toward Snarel, while Elkman addresses Hindman. "Let's git those animals t'gether, so we can be on our way." With a consenting nod, the storekeeper starts toward the back of the building, and Elkman follows.

Chapter 18

In front of Hindman's store, Amy sits on the edge of the travois by her unconscious uncle. She snugs a blanket around him and then shades his face from the sun. Gazing to the front porch, she sees McGredy, with his rifle rested across his lap, sitting in one of the rocking chairs. Not far away, in the shade of a low, scrubby tree, Bob Snarel sits whittling with a folding knife.

Eventually, Elkman and Hindman, leading the mounts, emerge from behind the store. Snarel sees them and scowls, as he uses his sharpened twig to pick his teeth. On the porch, McGredy stands from the rocker and proceeds down the steps to greet them. After Elkman ties the horses to the hitching rail, McGredy tilts his head toward Snarel. "What 'bout them other horses they brought along?"

Elkman shrugs, "We have no need of 'em."

"They're worth *somethin'* though, ain't they?"

Hindman steps up and offers, "Take the animals along, if ya want. Otherwise, I'll keep 'em here, and, if no one comes to make claim, I'll sell 'em."

Snarel folds his knife and tucks it into his vest pocket. "Oh, there'll be folks a' comin'..."

McGredy looks over, leaving the hammer of his rifle cocked as he points it in Snarel's direction. "Who'll be comin'?"

"Don't know. But, when word gets out 'bout yer escape, I reckon there'll be a healthy bounty put up fer yer capture."

The gambler scoffs, "For a scuffle at a pok'r table?"

Using the tip of the whittled stick, Snarel picks his teeth. "*And,* yer so-called doin's over in Wyomin'..."

McGredy protests, "That warn't us... It was *you.*"

The outlaw smiles. "Not as far as *they* know..."

His rifle pointed at Snarel, McGredy's anger simmers. He considers pulling the trigger to end the troublesome man, until Elkman puts out his hand and pushes the barrel down. "Leave it be... He's jest tryin' t'git ya riled."

McGredy turns and grimaces. "It's workin'... Don't know how much more of that fella I can stand."

Elkman glances at the instigator. "It gits t'be too much, we'll put a gag on 'im."

McGredy heaves a sigh and then smiles at the thought. "Not havin' to hear his mouth runnin' *would* be a nice relief." The gambler safely lets his rifle's hammer down. He then goes over to his horse and mounts up.

Elkman unties one of the other horses and hands the reins to Amy. "How's yer uncle?"

"He is passed out from the pain, so I tucked another bottle under his arm for when he wakes." She tosses the end of the reins over the neck of the horse, then slips a foot in the stirrup and climbs up.

Elkman hands her the lead line to her uncle's horse and then watches McGredy tuck his rifle across his lap and get situated in his saddle. He waves to Snarel and calls him over. "Time to go, Bob."

The outlaw gets to his feet, pats his hand on the folded knife in his vest pocket, and then saunters over to the horse. Taking the reins, he checks the cinch and climbs aboard. "Thank ya kindly fer the fine mount... Not quite as fresh as the ones I took from ya in Wyomin', but fine none-the-less."

Elkman quells his rising anger, as he glares at Snarel and reflects on the man's ill deeds. "You bin warned… One misstep, and we'll end ya fer good."

"Sure… Anythin' beats a lynch mob." With a half-grin, Snarel turns his horse away and notices McGredy with his rifle still pointed in his direction. He raises his hands mockingly. "Oh, no, no… Don't shoot me, Mista McGredy! I won't try t'escape. No, sirree." Snarel laughs and puts his hands down. As he watches Elkman go to his horse and take the lead for the mule with the stretcher, Snarel's eyes flicker with an evil glint. "Golly… Us ol' saddle pals t'gether again, with a pretty gal and a cripple along. Boy-howdy, this is gonna be somthin'…"

Chapter 19

As the afternoon sun sets behind the mountains, the group travels slowly, so as not to jostle the injured man on the travois. James Mitchell, with his bottle uncorked, is semi-conscious. Riding close beside him is his niece, with Snarel trailing them and McGredy bringing up the rear. Keenly observant of them, the outlaw is content to ride along peaceably.

Growing more disgruntled as they proceed further west, McGredy, rifle in hand, watches the prisoner. Trying to recall the route to the cabin, Elkman carefully picks his way along, leading them through wooded terrain toward higher ground. As the sun glows below the horizon, the riders crest a ridge and view the campsite below. Elkman halts his horse and looks directly behind at the pack animal hauling the stretcher and then to the others. "This is it..."

McGredy prods Snarel to ride ahead, so he can rein up beside Elkman for a chat. "Not sure if we were hopelessly lost or jest havin' a good look 'round."

"There's a reason this place ain't bin found by many."

Unimpressed, Amy looks down at the cliffside cabin and makeshift corral. "There's not much to find."

Elkman turns to look at her and then scratches his beard. "It's 'nough." Amy nods her consent, sighs, and glances down at her sleeping uncle. Elkman adjusts his hat, prods his horse, and gives a commanding tug on the lead line to the pack mule. The rest follow him down to the camp.

~*~

A fire inside an iron stove illuminates the dugout cabin. Snarel, with his hands tied in front of him, lounges with his back against a dirt wall. Amy sits on a chair, and her uncle is laid out on the only bed in the room.

McGredy, at the doorway, motions for Elkman to come outside. After glancing at Snarel, Elkman grabs a double-barreled shotgun, checks its load, and draws back both hammers before setting it next to Amy. "That fella moves from there, blast 'im. I have t'speak with Jefferson 'bout somethin'." He looks to Snarel, and the man smiles back with his corn-toothed grin. With a shake of his head, Elkman follows McGredy outside.

The only light, other than from the moon, is the flickering glow from the stove inside the cabin. McGredy steps back to the shadows, leans on his rifle and silently stares at him, until Elkman asks, "What is it, McGredy?"

"How long we gonna stay here?"

"I dunno… Until her uncle can ride. Maybe a month…"

"Some of us'll prob'ly be dead in a week."

His eyes adjusting to the dim light, Elkman can make out McGredy's sour expression. "Ya sick…?"

"I'm sick of losin' sleep, havin' ta keep one eye open on that kid-murderin' horse rustler."

Elkman tilts his head to glance in at Amy sitting next to her wounded uncle. "This isn't how I'd like it to be, either."

The gambler cradles his rifle on his arm and looks out to the darkened hills. "We might be clear of those that'll follow fer a short while, but we got the devil 'imself right here *with* us..." As McGredy continues, Elkman takes his tobacco from his vest and starts to roll a smoke. "It was bad 'nough keepin' a watch on 'im while we rode here, but if I let my guard down for jest a damn moment, he'll pounce and stick that foldin' knife right in my gizzard."

Elkman finishes with the tobacco and takes out a match. "Take it away from 'im, then."

"Won't matter… He'll find a stick, a rock, or somethin'. The point is, he's got murderin' on his mind, 'nd he'll git it done sooner or later, unless we git him first."

The matchstick flares, and Elkman lights his cigarette. "What d'ya suggest…? We jest kill 'im?"

McGredy peers in the cabin to see Snarel sitting there, staring at the loaded shotgun. "It's not somethin'

I'd *like* t'do, but, if'n ya got a dangerous animal, ya hafta put it down 'fore it hurts others... 'Cause, *it will.*"

Elkman thinks as he takes a drag, then blows the smoke. "I had my chance ta kill 'im in that saloon at Twin Fork Gulch. Didn't take it then, and I've lived to regret it."

"Ya can do it *now.*"

"I've killed men 'fore, but t'was in the act of self-defense. The thought of it ain't t'be taken lightly..."

"Well, how 'bout we give the gal's uncle enough of that Who-Hit-John, and he'll be glad t'do it."

Elkman lifts his chin and lets out another puff of smoke. "Ain't the right thing ta do..."

"So, we wait until he harms one of us? Or kills someone, and then we do it...? I don't like *that* idea."

"It's a matter for the law to handle."

Frustrated, McGredy gazes up at the night sky. "Law...? Ain't none of that here, and them kind flourish without it."

With the rolled cigarette pinched between two fingers, Elkman taps his own chest. "There's law of man inside o' here. Ya go 'gainst it, *yer* no better than *he* is."

McGredy groans in agreement and then shifts his rifle. "Maybe so, but if that son-of-a-bitch keeps smilin' like he does, I'm gonna knock his teeth in."

Elkman takes another drag and tosses his smoke away. "He's got it comin', alright." With that said, he turns and walks off toward the corral to check on the animals. McGredy watches him disappear into the darkness.

Chapter 20

The morning sky brightens, and a cook-fire crackles in the middle of the camp. Elkman squats next to the flames and lifts the lid off a pot to stir the contents. Behind him, near the corral, McGredy rolls out from his blanket and gets up. After sniffing, he coughs. "I could smell what you got cookin' in my dreams."

Elkman peers over at him. "Is that some kinda praise? We can eat well enough while we have it."

While stretching, McGredy looks over at Snarel, who appears to still be asleep. Then, he wanders to the cook-fire. "Keep up with that cookery 'nd any fellers lookin' fer us'll find the place easy 'nuff from followin' a scent on the breeze."

Elkman replaces the lid on the stew pot and then contemplates an idea that has come to mind. McGredy stands next to him, stares into the flames, and then glances over to where Snarel sleeps. "He stir any in the night?"

"Not that I saw."

"He's pretty confident we won't kill 'im, I guess."

"Could be..."

McGredy takes a knee next to Elkman, then leans in and pokes the fire with a stick. "Ya stay up all night watchin' 'im?"

"Mostly..."

"How long we gonna be doin' that?"

Elkman adds another piece of wood to the campfire. "That's what I've been thinkin' on."

"Yeah?"

"Us holed up here won't last."

"Agreed."

While gazing at the outlaw, Elkman shifts on his heels, and then looks back to McGredy. "Whether it's a lawman's posse or more of his kind, they'll find us eventually."

McGredy gestures to the cabin. "We could leave the girl ta care for her uncle and take 'im back to Wyomin' alone."

"That same thought has crossed my mind more'n once, but she wouldn't have it, most likely. Besides, how would it look if we came across some lawman or a posse?"

The gambler nods and ponders their situation. "Yeah... If she come all this way out here to see that he gets punished, she ain't gonna be convinced t'do otherwise. D'ya have a plan?"

"Not yet, but I'm workin' on one."

At the sound of movement from the cabin, they turn to see Amy step out with a steaming cup of coffee in each hand. She hands one to each of them. McGredy deeply sniffs the aroma and then has a sip. "Much obliged, ma'am."

"What plans are you two cooking up out here?"

McGredy averts his eyes to keep from revealing his intention of leaving her. "Jest makin' up some breakfast."

She looks to each of them, then admonishingly utters, "Smells like more than that to me."

Sheepishly, the gambler smiles at her. "Tomas here is the one with all the ideas."

She tilts her chin toward Elkman. "Don't you go and think of leavin' me with my uncle, b'cause I won't have it."

When she turns her stare back to McGredy, the gambler shakes his head. "No, ma'am! N'er even crossed our minds." With a guilty look, he glances at Elkman. "We wouldn't leave and take that bad character away from here to keep her safe, would we, Tomas?"

Elkman has a sip of his hot coffee and looks up at Amy. "I'm gonna have a scout around today. McGredy'll watch 'im. You keep close 'nd tend to yer uncle."

The gambler sits back on his haunches, eyes Elkman, and cradles his steaming cup in his hands. "Where ya goin'?"

Elkman stands and stretches his back. "I'll be 'round." After taking another sip of coffee, he heads toward the corral. Glancing back over his shoulder, he shouts, "Could be, I'll be gone a good while, so don't wait up for me."

~*~

Later, Elkman stands with his saddled horse, looking to the cook-fire, where McGredy eats from a plate of food set on the rifle laid across his lap. The gun points at Snarel, who still looks to be asleep. After filling another plate from the cookpot, Amy takes it to Elkman. "You should eat before you go."

He takes the plate and looks at her. "Thank ya."

Amy rubs the horse's neck, watches Elkman start to eat, and remarks, "McGredy says that you're gonna scout for tracks in case someone might have followed us."

The cowboy nods while he chews. "We need t'know what we'll be up against 'fore they come."

She watches him swallow, noticing the movement of his throat despite the unkempt beard. "Be careful..."

Scooping the remainder of the food off the plate and onto a biscuit, he takes a bite. Holding his biscuit, he hands the plate to Amy. "I ain't lookin' to git kilt..."

She moves in closer and reaches to touch his face. "You take care of yourself, Tomas Elkman. When you get back, we'll get to the task of cleaning you up some."

Cheeks flushed, he looks to see if anyone else heard her. Turning to his horse to hide his embarrassment, he mutters, "I'll be back soon 'nough..."

Amy moves backward, as Elkman steps up on his horse. He gazes down at her, gives a nod, and then rides over to the cook-fire to talk with McGredy. The gambler looks at Amy, then back up to Elkman, as the cowboy states, "Be gone a while. Don't let 'im outta yer sight."

At his being mentioned, Snarel, grinning in his usual way, wakes, gets to his feet, stretches, and walks over to them. "I'll keep a kerful watch on all of 'em."

Troubled by Snarel's confident demeanor, Elkman glances at the outlaw. Then, with a knowing nod to McGredy, he rides off.

Chapter 21

Elkman rides through the mountains with his rifle cradled across the saddle horn. As he scans the terrain for tracks, his steady gaze occasionally darts to the horizon in search of riders. After finding a concealed, elevated position that would allow him to watch the campsite from a distance, he dismounts.

He pulls the bridle from his horse and hobbles its front feet before sitting on the ground with his back against a tree. Rifle rested on his lap, Elkman takes out his tobacco pouch and rolling papers. He rolls a cigarette, lights it and takes a few puffs before relaxing his head back against the tree. Reluctantly, he heaves a sigh and then drifts off to sleep.

~*~

Inside the dugout cabin, James Mitchell, on the bed, shifts uncomfortably due to the constant aching of his wound. He notices Amy beside him and then reaches for the bottle of whiskey on the table. Concerned, his niece asks, "Are you *sure?* You *need* that to *last.*"

"Unless ya got somethin' better for the pain."

She shakes her head and scoots the bottle closer to him. "When that's finished, there's only *one* more."

He grabs the bottle, uncorks it and takes a long swig. "This'll have t'do."

Conflicted, Amy gazes to the bandage around his hip. She watches him take another big gulp and then turns to leave. "I'll be back later to check on you."

"I'll either be drunk or dead." Hearing the familiar swish of the bottle being upended, she pauses a moment, then steps out through door into the sunshine.

In the shade near the corral, McGredy sits staring out at the mountains, while Snarel dozes against a wooden fencepost. Walking over to stand near them, she looks at the corral where Elkman's horse is noticeably absent. She asks, "Where do you think he went?"

McGredy shrugs. "He's a hard one t'figger, at times... S'pose he's out there guardin' the camp from somewhere."

"When do you think he'll return?"

He smoothes the whiskers on his cheeks and turns to look up at her. "Who knows if he'll come back here tonight. He's a bit of a loner, if ya ain't took notice."

She murmurs, "He'll come back soon enough."

McGredy raises an eyebrow and then turns to the cabin. "How's yer uncle doin'?"

"He's in bad pain and drinking a lot to quell it."

Several corral posts over, Snarel blinks his eyes open. "Sure is a waste of whiskey, if ya ask *me.*" Amy is speechless, as Snarel continues, "He'll likely die from that wound."

McGredy points the rifle at Snarel. "Who asked ya?"

Snarel smirks and shrugs. "Jest a waste, that's all."

With a click, McGredy thumbs the hammer of his gun. "Keep yer mouth shut, or I'll shut it for ya." The outlaw grins, puts up both hands, and then mockingly covers his mouth. Trying his best to not let Snarel get under his skin, McGredy looks back to Amy. "Only time'll tell if he'll heal or not."

She scans the campsite and then looks up the hillside. "How much time do we have?"

McGredy turns to glare at Snarel, sitting smugly with his hands folded on his lap. "We got more time than this feller." Both stare at the outlaw, then exchange a glance, unsure.

~*~

The horse grazes, as Elkman rests his head back on the trunk of a tree. The animal steps on a twig, and the snap jolts Elkman awake. Rifle in hand, he sits upright, scans the area and carefully listens. Eventually satisfied that the sound came from his horse, he gazes toward the camp.

Elkman scans along the far ridges, then focuses below. First, he notices McGredy sitting in the shade near the cabin, then Snarel leaning back on a corral post. Elkman studies the remainder of the camp and notices

Amy standing just inside the cabin doorway. He lets his gaze wander over the terrain. Smelling the faint scent of the campfire, he looks to see if the smoke lingers above the tree line. Satisfied with his survey of the area, he dips his fingers into his vest pocket to pull out his tobacco and rolling papers.

Chapter 22

As evening sets, the cook-fire has died down, but a cast iron pot still hangs over the coals. Amy exits the cabin with a dirty plate and goes over to the campfire, where there is a pan of warm water for washing dishes. As she squats, she hears a horse approaching and turns to look.

"Hallo the camp… It's Tomas. I'm coming in."

Amy wipes the plate and stands, as Elkman rides nearer. He glances at her, nods his head, and then rides past to put his horse in the corral. She sees McGredy greet him, and they have a few quiet words before the gambler motions toward Snarel. Elkman peers back at Amy, as she scoops a portion of food onto the cleaned plate.

When they move to the cook-fire, they are received by Amy offering a plate of food to Elkman. "You must be hungry."

"That I am."

"Did you find anything out there?"

"No, not really…"

She curiously looks him over, glances at McGredy and then back to Elkman again. "Where did you go?"

He points to the hills. "Thereabouts…"

McGredy turns to watch Snarel standing by the corral, eyeing the horses. "I best git back to guard duty, or he'll bolt." As he passes by Elkman, he lowers his voice. "Remember what I said, n' think 'bout it."

"I'll come take over for ya after I've done ate."

Elkman squats on his heels, almost to his spurs, and lifts his plate of food to smell it. Amy watches, as McGredy supports his rifle across his chest and goes back to guard the prisoner. She turns back to Elkman and asks, "What did he suggest?"

Elkman adds a stick to the fire and then gazes up at her as he starts to eat. "He's not keen on stickin' around this camp and waitin' much longer."

She turns to the cabin and sighs. "None of us are."

"How's yer uncle?"

"Not well…"

Elkman stirs his plate. "I'm sorry…"

"Me, too…"

"When d'ya think he could travel?"

Unhopeful, she glances toward the dark cabin. Not yet ready to accept the reality of her uncle's condition, she asks, "Where did you go today?"

"Needed to have a look 'round."

Amy sighs. "I feel better when you're here."

"Always best not to have all yer eggs in one basket."

She looks across the revived coals of the campfire to see a cowboy that looks much different from how he looked on their first encounter. "Tomas... Do you remember the first time we talked?"

He looks up, forks another mouthful, chews a moment and then answers. "Yes..."

She stares at his beard and watches it move as he chews. Briefly, she considers her task to find and warn them to have been a waste of time. Amy looks around to be sure that no one is listening, then crouches down. "I was heartbroken to hear about my brother Kent being killed... But, when you didn't return to the ranch, I felt another sort of loss."

Elkman stares back at her while he chews and then scratches under his chin before responding. "I thought 'bout comin' back, but I didn't want to be the reminder of bad news. Heck, I didn't even know if you'd still *be* there."

"Where would I go?"

"Back east..."

She smiles at him. "I've been to those places already. Had a lot of fun, but I didn't belong."

He grins back. "That's how I feel 'bout *most* towns."

Amy glances at the horses in the corral and then back across the campfire to him. "How do you feel about ranch life?"

He pauses his eating, thinks, and stares back at her. "Dunno... It might be somethin' I could git used to."

"Maybe even grow to love...?"

"Perhaps..."

They share an intimate moment as they meet each other's gaze, until Elkman scratches his lip and resumes eating. Studying him, she finally asks, "Will you be up all night?"

He glances over at McGredy, who is binding Snarel's hands again after letting him urinate. Elkman nods, "I have'ta watch that feller till mornin'."

She stands and brushes her hands down the front of her riding skirt. "How about I give you a shave tonight?"

Elkman nearly chokes on a swallow of food, winces, and then touches his overgrown whiskers. "I don't have a razor."

"My uncle has one."

"Ya know how to shave a man?"

She grins. "I've done it before."

"Recent...?"

"I practiced some today, while he was asleep."

Elkman gulps. "How'd he turn out?"

"Handsome, with nary a nick..."

Elkman looks back at McGredy again, as the gambler finishes securing Snarel to the corral post. He turns back to her and speaks low. "Guess I *could* use some cleanup, since I missed the opportunity in town. Leave the mustache..."

"I *like* to kiss a man with a mustache."

Elkman blushes. "What's *that* got to do with it?"

Amused at his reticence, she nods with sincerity. "Yes... I will *leave* the mustache." Elkman tries not to ponder on her flirtatious comment and resumes eating.

As McGredy gets settled, Elkman turns back to Amy and takes note of her coy smile. "Let's wait till later, when they're both asleep, so I don't have to hear comments on the matter."

She brushes a stray lock of hair from her face and turns to the cabin. "That's fine… I'll get things ready."

Elkman watches her leave and then looks at the darkening evening sky. He watches for any unusual movement but only sees trees and the occasional flit of a bird in flight.

Chapter 23

A warm glow from the cabin stove illuminates the chamber. James Mitchell sleeps fitfully in the bed, while Snarel lies nearby with his hands tied to the bedpost. Across the room, on the floor, McGredy lies curled in his blanket, snoring softly.

Next to the stove, with his suspenders dropped around his waist, Elkman sits in his undershirt. Amy lifts a kettle of boiling water from the stovetop and pours some into a tin cup. Taking out a straight razor, she dips the blade in the hot water, lets it sit, and stands over Elkman. She sweeps the hair from his forehead and then touches him under his chin to tip his head. He eyes her nervously. "Ya say you've done this b'fore?"

"My uncle didn't complain."

With his head tilted back, Elkman turns a wary eye toward her uncle who is passed out from the pain and whiskey. "How *could* he…?"

She takes the warm razor from the cup and shushes him. "Be quiet now, so I don't slip." Putting the blade to his cheek, she gently presses the sharp edge against his skin and begins.

Elkman closes both eyes, trying to relax and not to flinch. As the whiskers are scraped away, he peeks at her and reminds, "Leave the moustache…"

"Quiet now…"

Amy shaves off another patch of beard, wipes the razor on a rag and dips the blade into the water again. Down at the foot of the bed, Snarel wakes and watches them in the dimness. The flickering light from the stove glints off his dark eyes and a hint of his yellow-toothed grin breaks through his scraggly, overhanging moustache.

~*~

In the morning chill, just as the sun begins to shine over the ridge, Elkman squats by the campfire. Not far from him, Snarel sits tied to a corral post. They listen to a rustle of activity inside the cabin. Eventually, McGredy comes through the door, with his morning routine of coughing to clear his chest.

The gambler walks to the cook-fire with his cup and reaches out for the coffee pot. After pouring a steaming serving, he squats opposite Elkman. McGredy's gaze studies Elkman, and a smile appears behind his cup as he takes a sip. "Huh… What happened to *you* last night?"

Elkman meets McGredy's amused expression and then has a drink from his own cup. "Nothin'..."

"Hardly... Ya bin slick'd up 'nd put claim to."

Elkman touches his clean-shaven cheek, then glances to the cabin where Amy still rests inside. "It needed doin'."

The gambler scratches his own, rough-bearded cheek. "She didn't offer *me* no barberin'."

With a soft grunt, Elkman smiles from behind his cup. "Ya look jest fine with a beard."

McGredy coughs. "Not *near* as pretty as *you* look now." He looks past Elkman toward Snarel and adds, "Ya plan to be ridin' off again today?" After receiving an affirming nod, McGredy continues. "Ya know, I'm startin' to git the feelin' that we're some kinda bait on display here the way ya light a fire, git things brewin', 'n then take yer leave."

Elkman takes a sip of coffee and wipes his moustache. "Jest be ready in case somethin' does happen. I spoke with her, and she doesn't think her uncle can travel for some time."

"Did ya consider what I proposed?" When Elkman offers another nod, McGredy blows steam from his cup. "Well...? Whadya think 'bout it?"

"It'll be a few days."

Looking at Snarel again, the gambler shakes his head. "Few days is all he's *got*, as far as *I'm* concerned."

Elkman takes one last swallow of his coffee and tosses the dregs on the ground. He sets the empty cup by the fire, stands, and looks at his horse in the corral, saddled and ready. "I'll be back tonight to spell ya on watchin' him."

The gambler looks up at Elkman and grumbles. "Fine..." He watches Elkman go to the corral, mount, and then ride off. McGredy's attention diverts to the cabin, and he notices Amy standing in the doorway. Their gazes briefly connect, before she backs from the entryway and disappears inside.

~*~

Several men on horseback fan-out through the trees, searching for a trail. A dark-skinned tracker in a fringed, buckskin shirt stops his horse and steps down to examine the ground. After studying the tracks, he calls out and the nearest rider trots closer.

There is a brief exchange, and the tracker points in the direction that the trail takes. The other riders gather around him and follow, as he leads them further into the mountains. One of them is the one who fled the fight at Hindman's store.

Chapter 24

Amy steps out of the cabin holding a fresh cup of coffee. Glancing at the cook-fire at the center of camp, she watches the smoke waft skyward. Then, she walks to the corral and hands McGredy the cup. He takes it and gives the contents a sniff. "Thank ya kindly, ma'am…"

She wipes her hands over her skirt and turns to Snarel. The prisoner stares back at her until she finally looks away. Amy watches McGredy blow the steam and then sip the coffee. She asks, "Where do you think he went today?"

"Prob'ly same as yesterday…"

Amy gazes out at the far ridge. "It's so *quiet*…"

McGredy wipes some dribbles of coffee from his beard. "I imagine that's why certain folks like it out in nature so well." He glances back, feeling uneasy speaking in front of Snarel.

Amy takes notice of the distrustful glare and comments, "He mentioned you had a plan."

"Of sorts…"

"I imagine my uncle would be upset, but he doesn't have much say in the matter, as he is in and out of consciousness."

McGredy lifts his cup for another sip. "Sorry 'bout him."

So as not to weep, Amy clenches her jaw and turns away. On the ridge, she spots a single rider and her pulse quickens. "He looks to be back already…" But, before she can say anything more, another rider appears, followed by yet another, and her heart sinks.

McGredy follows her gaze and sees the mounted men. "Ah, damn…"

Snarel looks up to the ridge and grins with satisfaction. "Guess he found 'im some friends."

McGredy pulls back the hammer on his rifle and points the barrel at Snarel. "If'n we have any difficulties with them, yer the first to git a bullet." After quickly taking another gulp, he sets the coffee cup aside and gets up. He cradles the rifle on his forearm, keeping it pointed at Snarel, and whispers to Amy. "Go inside to yer uncle 'nd stay there." When she is reluctant, he gives her a stern glare. Watching the riders descend upon the camp, he counts seven of them. As they approach, none of them have weapons out, but each man is equipped for a fight. The leader wears a badge, but the riders behind look to be made up of a civilian posse.

They stop and address McGredy. "Hallo the camp!"

Rifle still pointed at Snarel, McGredy calls them in. "Come ahead… What kin I do fer ya?"

The riders fan out as the lawman rides toward McGredy. "We are in search of some fugitives from justice that done some killin' o'er yonder at Hindman's Tradin' Post."

McGredy's studying gaze goes to the rider directly behind the lawman, and he recognizes him from the store. Scanning the others, he assesses their character individually. "We do have a prisoner who we plan to take to Wyoming."

Snarel's associate whispers to the lawman, and they look to the prisoner tied to the corral. The lawman pats his pocket. "I have an affidavit. May I take it out?"

McGredy nods. "Go ahead."

The lawman takes out the document and unfolds it. "We're lookin' for two males who escaped lawful custody." The rider eases alongside him, leans over to whisper, and then points at McGredy. The lawman offers the sworn paper. "Would you care to have a look at this?"

McGredy nods to the one pointing at him and grumbles, "If it has anythin' t'do with that feller there, I'm not interested in what that claim-jumper has to say."

The lawman looks to the corral and counts the horses. "Who else is hereabouts?"

McGredy tilts his head toward the cabin. "There's a man inside there."

"Could you ask him to come out?"

"He's sleepin'."

At a standstill, the lawman looks around, then to Snarel. "Do *you* have anythin' to say?"

The outlaw looks at the rifle directed at him and shrugs. "Like he says, I'm a prisoner."

The lawman turns in the saddle to see that the posse has spread through the camp. He pivots to McGredy and offers, "How 'bout we take this conversation to the nearest town, where we can git all this figured out?"

McGredy stands firm. "How 'bout y'all ride on…"

Looking at Snarel, who shakes his head, the rider then leans over and hisses orders at the lawman. The officer hastily waves him away, then folds and tucks the paper into his vest. As the lawman opens his coat to reveal a sidearm, he offers, "I'm afraid we have to insist that *you,* your *friend,* and the *prisoner,* come with us."

McGredy determines the odds, as he eyes each of the men to see if they're ready for a fight. None, except the rider directly beside the lawman, seems too eager. "If we go with ya, it'll only be our word 'gainst theirs."

"If you don't come peaceable, we'll use force."

McGredy keeps his rifle pointed at Snarel, while sidestepping a few paces closer to him. "This feller escaped justice once b'fore, and it won't happen again."

"Be reasonable man. We don't want to have this fight." The lawman lifts his hand as a signal, and the riders in the camp all take out their weapons.

McGredy makes sure the barrel of his rifle is pointed directly at Snarel and waits. He glances at the cocked hammer, puts his finger on the trigger, and then glares at the lawman. "I'm ready fer it, if'n *you* are…"

The lawman pleads, "You'll die, sir…"

As a woman's voice calls from the cabin, they all turn. "He surely won't be the only one!"

Amy levels the double-barreled shotgun toward them. The lawman shakes his head. "And, who is *this…?*"

McGredy smugly answers, "She's kin to the boy this fella murdered in Wyomin'."

Realizing that they are at an impasse, the lawman holds everyone at bay. "Let's settle this civilized…"

McGredy nods. "I'm in agreement with that."

"Then, lower your weapons."

The gambler shakes his head. "Nope… *Yer* the guest. Go ahead and put up *yer* guns, 'n *then* we kin talk."

The lawman looks around and, with an affirmative nod, he gestures for his men to holster their guns and stand down. As they comply, Snarel glares at his associate and hollers, "Dammit…! *Shoot* this bastard already!!!"

Chapter 25

The man beside the lawman lifts his pistol and fires off a shot. The bullet tears across McGredy's arm, spinning him sideways, nearly tumbling him to the ground. To defend himself, McGredy pivots and fires at the rider. The return shot misses, hitting the lawman dead center instead. His sidearm still holstered, the officer tumbles from the saddle, and lies sprawled on the ground.

In an instant, the fighting has commenced. Hurriedly, Snarel's associate takes another shot, missing again, and Amy fires off a barrel of the shotgun, blasting him from his horse. When they see the lawman, and the other rider gunned down, the posse brandish their weapons again.

McGredy quickly assesses the situation and dives for cover behind a boulder near where the cliff meets the corral. Several bullets slam into the rock face and chips of stone shower down from the bluff as the posse unleashes a hail of gunfire. Most of the horses are rearing or kicking in panic.

The buckskinned tracker holds tight to his frantically bucking mount, until he flies off, hits the ground hard, and is knocked unconscious. Another rider hastily dismounts and fires a shot at the cabin. As the bullet tears into the doorjamb near her head, Amy jumps back and fires the other barrel of the scattergun before ducking further inside for cover. Undeterred, she breaks the shotgun open, ejects the spent shell casings and loads two fresh ones.

~*~

At the sound of distant gunfire, Elkman's eyes pop open. He looks to his nearby saddled horse and then down at the camp to see the telling puffs of smoke. "Aww, *dammit...*"

Elkman stands up, grabs his rifle and races to his mount. He tosses the split reins over the animal's neck, tightens the saddle's cinch strap and remembers to unhobble the front legs. Gunfire continues, as Elkman tucks away the hobbles and then slips a boot into the stirrup. Rifle in hand, Elkman's seat barely hits the saddle, before he gives the horse a kick and races toward the camp.

~*~

McGredy can barely peek out, let alone shoot, as bullets ricochet off the wall behind him. Dusted with shards of rock, he hunkers down, until there is a brief break in the skirmish. He peers out to see Snarel tugging at the bindings on his wrists. "Bob...! Move from that damn spot, n' I'll put a bullet in ya!!!"

Snarel glances over at the gambler's position, sees that he's pinned down, and keeps pulling at the rope securing him. "Go roll apples, McGredy! We'll see who gets a bullet first!" Infuriated, McGredy tries to get a shot, but the opposing gunfire is too heavy.

From inside the cabin, Amy pokes the barrels of her shotgun out through the doorway and squeezes both triggers. The blast sends a pair of smoke rings rolling across the camp, as the members of the dismounted posse scatter for cover. Reloading, she notices the buckskin-clad tracker laid out on the ground not far from the dead lawman and the rider she shot. Aiming the shotgun outside again, she fires.

What remains of the posse hides behind rocks and trees at the edge of camp, watching as their horses scatter to the hills. One of them, gawking at the laid-out bodies, whines in protest, "*Gol-dammit...* This isn't what *I* signed up fer!"

Next to him, another posse member fires his pistol. While taking aim, he cocks his gun again. "Then, what was ya *thinkin'* when he told ya to bring along yer shootin' iron?"

The other peeks out at the dead lawman and mutters, "*He* sure didn't 'xpect to git kilt, I'll tell ya *that.*"

"That's what happens to a fella when ya git to jawin' first 'nd shootin' second."

They turn their attention toward the tracker, who doesn't have a visible wound and looks to be still breathing. The man complains, "Without that scout, we can't even find our way home."

"He's not dead. Jest looks ta be playin' possum…"

"We ain't goin' anywheres with him like *that!*"

The men both fire their guns, alternating their aim between McGredy behind the rock, and Amy inside the cabin. Another posse member scurries up behind them to peer over their shoulders. "This ain't good… What're we gonna do 'bout the feller tied to the fence?"

While reloading his handgun, one of them remarks, "With any luck, he gits shot *accidental-like,* so we don't hav'ta *deal* with 'im. This *whole thing* has gone *bad.*"

The one who just joined them levers his rifle and takes careful aim. "Hey… I could pick him off right *now.*"

While snapping the side-gate of his loaded pistol closed, one of them grumbles, "At least wait till we take care of them others first."

Holding his revolver close to his chest, the other posse member reluctantly turns and hunkers down behind the rock. "I don't like this… We're *all* gonna git kilt…"

Chapter 26

Amy fires the shotgun again and breaks open the breach to clear the empties. She reaches into a cloth sack to find her last two shells and plunks them into the gun. Realizing that this is the end of her ammunition, she puts the shotgun aside and searches the cabin for another weapon.

In the corner, by the bed, she spots her uncle's rifle and rushes toward it. As she picks the gun up, a man dashes into the cabin and grabs her from behind. Kicking and screaming, she tries to free herself from his grasp as he drags her outside.

The gunfire suddenly ceases, and McGredy pokes his head up to see why. He sees Amy being dragged from the cabin and lifts his rifle to take a shot. The wound on his arm causes him to wince as he adjusts the stock to his chest and takes aim. Suddenly, McGredy senses someone step up behind him, and when the hammer clicks back on a pistol, the gambler turns to see who it is. Free from his bonds, Snarel remarks with a grin. "*This* is a familiar sight, ain't it?"

Quickly calculating the odds of being able to turn and fire before Snarel shoots, McGredy lowers the aim of his rifle. The outlaw gives a motion for him to lay it on the ground. "Drop that shooter, or *I* drop *you*." McGredy lets go of the rifle, letting it fall against the boulder, and Snarel laughs spitefully. "Should've taken a chance… Now *you'll* git what *I* had comin'." With the barrel of his gun, he motions for the gambler to stand.

As Amy is forcefully dragged away from the cabin, McGredy, at gunpoint, is ushered from cover near the corral. The surviving posse members are now gathered at the fire pit, gazing around. Someone asks, "What now…?"

Not sure if he should holster his pistol or not, one of them answers, "*I* don't know… I ain't paid to do the *thinkin'*."

Pushing McGredy before them, Snarel addresses the puzzled faces. "Git a rope. We're gonna have us a lynchin'." The posse exchanges looks of uncertainty while gazing at the lawman lying dead on the ground.

Another one speaks up. "What 'bout the woman?"

Snarel turns and smiles right at her. "She's a part of it..." He gestures to his dead associate killed by the shotgun blast, and then to the unconscious tracker sprawled out nearby. "…and, should be punished likewise."

One of the men brings over a horse, removes a coil of rope from the saddle, and hands it over. Snarel throws out some line to make a loop, then looks around for a proper tree. "We best do it quick, cause there's another of 'em out there yet." While still holding his gun on him, Snarel raises the loop end of the rope over McGredy's neck and cinches it tight. He leads him to a tree and throws the remainder of the coil over a branch. Gesturing to the horse and then Amy, he instructs the posse. "Git that woman up in the saddle, and we'll do her the same."

Someone asks, "With jest one horse…?"

Snarel sneers. "Sometimes, ya jest hav'ta git creative." Promptly, he tosses the length of rope at them and orders, "Loop that rope 'round her neck 'n tie her hands to the saddle."

Reluctant to take unlawful actions, but not having the courage to protest, the posse members do as they are instructed. Though Amy squirms and fights, her hands are firmly fastened to the saddle horn. She looks at McGredy, with a rope around his neck, standing unusually quiet and gazing off to the hills.

As Snarel walks past, she leans over and spits on him. He stops to wipe his cheek and then stares up at her with his piercing gaze. "Now, *that* wasn't very lady-like."

"Go to hell."

"Soon 'nough. But, ladies first…" He turns to McGredy. "Things sure didn't turn out how *you'd* like, eh McGredy?"

Holding back her tears, Amy pleads, "Don't *do* this…"

McGredy kicks at the outlaw with his boot, but finds he is just out of reach. With a laugh, Snarel raises his pistol in the air and cocks the hammer. But, before he squeezes the trigger, another shot rings out and the horse Amy is on takes a step backward and falls to the ground, dead. Tied to the saddle, Amy hops to the side as they fall.

Snarel looks to where the gunshot came from and sees Elkman, on horseback with rifle in hand, charging at the camp. Snarel promptly turns his pistol toward McGredy and fires. One of the posse, jumping into action and heading for cover, passes between Snarel and McGredy just as the shot is fired. The bullet hits the man's chest, and he tumbles to the ground with his gun held out. The gambler and the outlaw both glance at the weapon and, before Snarel can get off another shot, McGredy charges, delivering him a swift kick to the knee.

At the end of his tether, McGredy attempts to stomp Snarel but can't get close enough without choking himself. "Gol-dammit, I'll kill ya *this* time, Bob!"

Rolling away from the gambler's reach, Snarel comes up wincing and holding his injured knee. After gasping a breath, he cocks his pistol and extends his arm to take aim.

Chapter 27

A blast from the shotgun knocks a posse member off his feet, and everyone turns to look at the cabin doorway, where Amy's uncle stands with a smoking gun. Snarel shifts his aim over, snaps off a shot, and hits his target. The bullet pierces James Mitchell's chest. Before he crumples, he directs the other barrel of the scattergun at Snarel and lets loose.

Snarel dives away, as shotgun pellets kick up dirt. McGredy tries to get slack in the hanging rope and loosen the cinched loop around his neck. As the last surviving posse member grabs for the line connecting Amy and McGredy, Elkman charges at him and shoots the man down in his tracks.

Elkman whirls his horse around to see Snarel climb to his feet and point his gun at McGredy. He levers a fresh round into his rifle, but as he takes the shot, his horse skitters sideways and the bullet misses. Snarel glances at Elkman and then focuses on his intended target.

With his hands tied and the rope still around his neck, McGredy turns to see Snarel aiming a gun at him once again. The gambler sees no means of escape, so he faces his adversary and awaits his imminent fate. Before Snarel can pull the trigger, the previously knocked-out tracker sits up and sweeps the gunman's feet out from under him. Snarel falls and the stray shot smashes into the rocky cliff.

When Snarel attempts another shot, the tracker hammers his fist to the side of his head, knocking him out cold. The tracker gets to his feet, brushes himself off, and looks at the dead lawman and posse members.

Elkman steers his horse over to Amy and McGredy. Astonished, McGredy stares, first at the unconscious outlaw, and then at the man who did it. *"Why…?"*

After using his boot to nudge the gun from Snarel's grip, the tracker grabs his hat from the ground. "It ain't right shootin' a man jest b'fore he's t'be lynched." Awestruck, McGredy continues to stare, as the man pulls down his neckerchief to display a rope scar on his neck. "Take it from me, I *knows*."

McGredy tugs at the rope that still binds his wrists. "Thank you… What's yer name, sir?"

"Dobkins… Maxwell Dobkins…" He steps to McGredy, looks at his bound hands, and uses a knife to cut him loose.

"Thank you, Mister Dobkins."

Elkman steps down from his horse and draws his own knife to cut Amy free from the saddle. Then, he lifts the hanging rope from around her neck. After a quick look of gratitude, she rushes to her uncle in the cabin doorway.

Massaging his sore wrists, McGredy turns to Elkman. "What took ya so long, pard?"

Elkman scans the carnage and then looks at the discarded noose at the gambler's feet. "Whad'ya mean…? Looks t'me like I was jest in time."

McGredy follows his gaze to the line going up and over the tree branch and then leading down to the dead horse. "Why'd ya shoot the *horse?"*

Elkman gestures to Snarel. "Was jest aimin' ta shoot *him,* 'nd the durned critter dropped its head at the wrong moment."

"What if ya'd hit *him,* and that horse *bolted!?"*

Elkman slips cartridges from his gunbelt and reloads. "Figured it'd take more'n one to lift you off the ground."

McGredy gawks at the hanging rope and the dead horse. "My *body* maybe, but not my *head!"*

Elkman briefly thinks on it and nods in agreement, as he slips another cartridge into the side gate of his Winchester. "Huh… Didn't think of it that way. Yer prob'ly right."

Incredulous, the gambler stares at Elkman, until they hear a wail of grief coming from the cabin.

Chapter 28

Just beyond the camp, the men stack rocks for a burial mound. The members of the posse are lumped into a common grave, but James Mitchell's spot has his own separate pile of stones. Elkman watches McGredy working alongside Dobkins, and turns to the cabin as Amy steps out.

Tears streaming down her cheeks, she holds a letter clutched to her chest. Her gaze drifts to Snarel, who is once again tied to the corral post. The look of sadness turns to contempt as she considers the resulting casualties. She walks over and McGredy stands to greet her. "How ya holdin' t'gether, ma'am?"

Touching a hand to her teary eye, she smiles at him. "Thank you for doing this for my uncle…" She wipes her cheek. "I suppose you did the same for my brother."

Elkman removes his hat to wipe sweat from his brow. "It's a task not taken lightly." As her gaze lingers on him, tears continue to swell in her eyes. Alongside them, while the tracker continues to add to the burial mounds, Elkman turns to him. "Should be 'nough to keep the critters from diggin' at 'em." Curious, Elkman addresses the scout. "Dobkins, was it?"

"Yes, sir…"

After brushing the dirt from his vest, McGredy studies the kerchief fitted around the tracker's neck. "Were ya a slave?"

"We's *all* a slave t'*somethin'*. I'm a *free* man now."

Concerned, Amy gestures toward the common grave. "How well did you know these men?"

Dobkins looks to the only other single gravesite, next to her uncle's, which he personally set aside for the dead lawman. "That fella there was my only *real* friend… Until ya *kilt* 'im." Dobkins turns to look at McGredy, who stands uneasy under the man's discerning stare.

McGredy touches the bandaged wound on his arm. "Was an unfortunate accident." Remorseful, McGredy heaves a sigh and takes a step back.

Dobkins turns his piercing glare to Snarel. "Yes, it was, and I know who's t'blame fer it."

Amy notices the accusatory look toward Snarel and sees the scout in a new light. She asks, "What are your plans now?"

He brushes his calloused hands together and takes a moment to evaluate the curious group of folks before him. "Well, I was thinkin', if ya let me stick with ya, I'd like t'see that man answer fer what he done here this day."

Placing his hat back on, Elkman adjusts the brim. "Wyoming Territory is a far piece, and that's where we plan to take him to pay for his misdeeds."

Dobkins looks at Elkman. "I gots nowhere else t'be… Some folks acquire a mess a debts that have t'be paid fer."

Elkman nods in reply. "We all do in our own way."

Not wanting to ruminate on his own past, McGredy grabs his rifle and walks to the corral. "I'll take the first watch." Turning to Elkman, he adds, "That is, if our plan is to still head out in the mornin'?"

Elkman glances at Amy and then back to McGredy. "First light…" After watching the gambler get settled on guard, Elkman addresses Dobkins. "I'm sorry 'bout yer friend."

The scout nods. "Me, too…"

"I cain't help but think ya might have a score to settle over the matter."

Dobkins shakes his head. "Nope…"

"Good, then… Yer welcome to come along with us." Elkman turns to Amy and glances down at the paper still clutched in her hand. "What's that?"

Another glistening stream of tears pour down her cheeks, as she recollects the letter. "It's a note from my uncle… He wrote it a few days ago, when he still had some clarity."

Elkman understands her need for comfort at this difficult time, but he is not sure how to help her. He looks over to her uncle's grave. "I hope it helps ya to find some peace."

She clutches the letter tighter to her chest and utters, "Tomas… I need to have a conversation with you privately." Overhearing the request, Dobkins tips his hat to them and drifts off to check on the horses. As the afternoon's last rays of sun slip behind the mountains, Elkman, mystified, stares at Amy, uncertain of what she has in store for him.

Chapter 29

"What's it mean?" The glow of the cabin's stove illuminates Elkman's features, as he sits on a stool across from Amy. Rocking back in a chair, she lowers the letter to her lap.

After staring at him for a moment, she bluntly states, "Not having any children of his own, it says that my uncle wants me to take ownership of his property, but implies that you are to be an important part of it."

"Why *me…?*"

"He respected you."

"There are good ranch foremen 'round those parts that'll tend to yer property better'n me."

"He wanted *you.*"

Elkman looks down at his feet, over at the flickering fire in the stove, and then out the doorway to where the others are. "I dunno… I have places t'be."

"Where…?"

Hesitating, he looks back at her and tries to be tactful. "Don't know, 'xactly, since I haven't *bin* there yet."

With a knowing gaze, she ignores his excuse. "Tomas, I'm not going to tie you down or try to keep you from living the life you want." She folds the letter and places it on the table. "My uncle offered you the opportunity to be part of something. It's up to you if you choose to take it."

Elkman looks away from her and fixes his gaze on the near darkness outside the doorway. With a sigh, he murmurs, "He was a good man, and I will strongly consider his request." After he grabs his rifle, he stands up. "I need to spell McGredy. We can talk more when the business at hand is finished." Holding her emotion, Amy nods and watches Elkman leave.

Left alone, Amy hears Elkman's steps going to the corral. She looks around the cabin, obviously set up for a bachelor, and glances to the bed where she had cared for her uncle. Suddenly, a deep sadness sweeps over her, and she turns from the glow of the firelight as tears stream down her cheek.

~*~

At daybreak, horses are saddled, and gear is packed. With his hands tied, Snarel is put up on a horse by McGredy. He smiles down at the gambler. "Betcha didn't think we'd be ridin' t'gether like this again…"

Trying to not let the man irritate him, McGredy rubs his sore neck and double-checks the ties on Snarel's wrists. Humoring him, McGredy states, "Could well be our last..."

As Dobkins mounts, McGredy glances to his own horse. The scout seems to know what he's thinking and kindly offers, "Go on... I'll watch 'im for ya."

McGredy notes that the tracker is unarmed, and nods as he goes over to his mount. He climbs into the saddle and then steers his horse over to where Elkman finishes with the mule. "Hey there, Tomas..."

At first, wondering who is guarding the prisoner, Elkman looks at McGredy, then past him to the tracker. "Yeah, what is it, McGredy?"

"I was ponderin' somthin'."

"Yeah...? You 'bout ready to leave here?"

McGredy grunts and pats dust off the sleeve of his coat. "Don't have anythin' with me but what I'm wearin', so bein' ready t'go ain't much."

Finished with the panniers, Elkman takes hold of the mule's lead rope and heads over to his horse. He looks around for Amy and sees her horse tied off at the front of the cabin. "When she's ready to go, we'll start on the trail eastward."

McGredy tilts his head toward the dark-skinned scout mounted next to Snarel. "What about *him?*"

Elkman looks over and studies the tracker's features. "He seems intent on comin' with us."

"Yeah... But, d'ya *trust* 'im?"

Elkman considers Dobkins' friendly behavior thus far. "He's got no sympathy for that man, but ya *did* kill his *friend.*"

McGredy nods apologetically. "Yeah... I did at that, and I am sorry fer it." He scratches his beard. "I was thinkin' we should give 'im a gun to help us watch over our prisoner."

Elkman considers the request and scans his saddle gear. He reaches behind the cantle to pull out the shotgun that was secured with his bedroll and offers it to McGredy. "It's loaded. Would come off best if *you* trusted 'im with it."

The gambler nudges his horse up alongside Elkman, takes the gun and puts it across his lap. He glances at Dobkins, then looks back to his partner. "I've done *dumber* things."

Elkman hides a playful grin. "Yaugh, ya prob'ly have." In return, McGredy casts a scolding gaze at Elkman, before he turns his horse away and rides over to Dobkins

Chapter 30

As McGredy moves past him, Snarel's stare lingers on the sawed-off shotgun. The gambler stops beside the tracker, and they sit silently, until Dobkins asks, "We's 'bout ready t'go?"

"Yeah... Jest 'bout..."

They watch Amy step out from the cabin and mount up. Dobkins looks at the scattergun laid across McGredy's saddle and misinterprets its meaning. "Don't need ta worry 'bout me. I's along fer the ride 'cause I gots nowhere else t'be."

The gambler takes the gun from his lap and offers it to him. Surprised, Dobkins peers down at the firearm. "Mista... Heck, ya trust me 'nough ta give me dat?"

McGredy's gaze flits over to Snarel and then back again. "I trust *you* a whole lot more'n *him*."

Dobkins takes the gun and perches the stock on his hip. "Could be I'll blast da both of ya..."

McGredy nods understandingly and cracks a wide grin. "Do me a favor and shoot *him* first."

In return, Dobkins' expression lights up, and he flashes a beaming smile. "Ya'sir... I'll be sure t'do that when I do."

Now puzzled to his intent, McGredy looks warily at the scattergun in the man's capable hands. "I cain't change what's happened. If'n I could, we wouldn't be in this durned fix." Nearby, Snarel listens while keeping an eye on the gun.

Dobkins remarks, "Bad things do happen, and the only thing t'do is move on best ya can." Elkman and Amy mount up, as Dobkins continues. "In da recent doin's, dat gal has lost more'n any of us."

McGredy thinks back on the death of young Kent and the pain it must have put on the family. He lowers his gaze in reverence and then looks at Dobkins. "She's endured the loss of *several* kin in this affair." He notices Elkman casting a glance at them and waving them along. As they ride out of the camp, McGredy motions for Snarel to ride ahead and for Dobkins, holding the shotgun, to follow.

~*~

The riders travel eastward, following a winding trail through the mountain. At the rear of the procession, McGredy exchanges a look with Dobkins and then rides ahead to speak with Elkman. He approaches him on the side opposite to where Amy rides and leans over to ask, "Are we plannin' to stop at that waystation again?"

Elkman shakes his head and keeps his gaze fixed on the horizon. "No... I don't reckon it'd be safe for us."

McGredy nods in agreement and glances behind. "Dobkins and I've bin talkin' and figured the same."

Surprised, Elkman inquires, "Sounds right friendly... What else ya been talkin' 'bout?"

"He thinks there'll be others that come after us."

"And, why's that, d'ya think?"

"Some of them fellers had well-liked relations in town, and when they don't come back, they'll git to lookin' for 'em." Elkman nods, noticing that Amy is listening. McGredy adds, "Could be a while, but they'll find what was left eventually."

"They'll either leave it be for what it is, or come after the ones they feel are responsible"

"Dobkins says that friend of his was much admired. Most likely, some'll come after and find what happened."

Elkman glances back at Dobkins to see him riding with the scattergun pointed at Snarel. He turns back to McGredy. "We've got supplies 'nough to stay clear of settled areas awhile. Best thing to do is steer 'round 'em till we reach Wyoming."

They ride a bit and McGredy glances at their prisoner. "Yeah, I guess that's the best way to travel fer now."

"What's botherin' you?"

With a heavy sigh, McGredy pats his empty vest pocket. "I ain't had a game of cards fer quite a spell now."

"Feelin' itchy...?"

"Jest don't want t'lose my luck."

Amused, Elkman questioningly tilts his head. "McGredy, what's happened of late that you consider *lucky?*"

The gambler cracks a grin and drops his horse back. "Well, I ain't *dead* yet, 'n *that's* pretty lucky."

Elkman turns to watch McGredy retake his position alongside Dobkins and Snarel. He exchanges an amused look with Amy, and they continue onward.

Chapter 31

Dobkins and McGredy sit watching Snarel, as Amy prepares a meal over a small cookfire. After tending to the horses, Elkman returns to camp and stops at the edge of the firelight. "Don't believe there's a settlement 'round for a hundred miles, but I still git the feelin' of bein' on display."

Dobkins looks beyond Elkman to the darkening sky. "We's in Indian territory... They's watchin' us, alright..."

Sitting up, McGredy reaches to grab his rifle. "Indians...? What sorta tribes are hereabouts?"

The tracker takes a moment to think and then answers. "Bannocks and Shoshone..."

Continuing to scan the horizon, Elkman steps closer. "Are they the kind t'worry 'bout?"

"Sheep-eater Indians... Mostly peaceful-livin', less'n ya disturb their way of life."

McGredy lays his rifle across his lap and glares at Snarel. "We've enough trouble on our hands with *him* along without needin' to disturb the locals."

Elkman considers the horses tied to a picket line just at the edge of the campsite. "Ya dealt with these natives much?"

"Some..."

"Any suggestions...?"

"Leave 'em be."

After taking another wary glance around, Elkman moves to a spot by the fire. "I guess that's good advice for encounters with jest 'bout anyone."

Amy hands Elkman a plate of food, as McGredy scans the hills surrounding the camp. The gambler smoothes his hand over the stock of his rifle and shakes his head. "I don't like it..."

As he is served a plate, Dobkins nods gratefully. "No honor to be had slittin' one's throat in the night."

"Honor, hell... I don't have these kinds of problems when I'm in town at a card table."

Elkman scoops up a mouthful of food, and then adds, "Playin' the last town, ya ended up in jail."

McGredy shoots him a guarded look. "Who asked ya? Ya ain't done none better."

"I'd rather take my chances out here."

Served last, Snarel, with his hands tied, holds his plate. His shifty eyes scan the ones in camp, and then he peers out into the unknown. "N'er know how things might turn out dealin' with the savage locals." As everyone turns to him, he cracks a grin and starts to eat.

McGredy takes a bite and grumbles under his breath. "Maybe they'll take ya off our hands and finish ya fer good, like they should'a done b'fore..."

The captive smirks. "We'll see who finishes who."

Elkman turns to the prisoner. "Quiet now, or we'll put a sack o'er yer head." Snarel picks at his food, reveling in McGredy's obvious irritation.

~*~

The clear sky brightens just before dawn. In the morning chill, the ashes from the night's fire let off wisps of smoke. McGredy stirs under his blanket, opens his eyes, and looks out from the camp to see a man horseback silhouetted on the hill. The native sits with his back straight, his feet dangling, and a blanket wrapped around his shoulders.

Quicky surveying the camp, McGredy takes note that their horses remain undisturbed. In the dim light, he turns to look at Elkman, who observes while leaning back on his saddle. He then looks over at Snarel, who grins impishly back at him. Elkman lifts a finger to his lips signaling him to keep quiet. Uneasy, but still in need of rest, McGredy glances at the Indian, then shifts under his blanket and lies back down.

An hour later, McGredy sits up, looks around the camp, and now sees a pair of horseback figures watching them. Noticing Dobkins packing up his gear, he turns to Elkman, points, and cusses. "Dammit... *Now* there's *two* of 'em."

Dobkins fastens his saddlebags and looks to McGredy. "Two that we kin see… There's prob'ly more'n *that* around."

McGredy peels off his blanket, tucks his pant legs into his boot tops and scoots over to Elkman. "I was okay with jest one of 'em comin' to visit, but now they seem to be multiplyin'. What's yer thought on this, pard?"

"They've jest been watchin' us."

"Well, what're we gonna to do 'bout it?"

Elkman takes a bite of a cold, hard biscuit and chews. "Nothing to be done…"

Always trying to improve the odds of a dubious situation, the gambler looks to Snarel and suggests, "Maybe we offer 'em that feller as a gift, and they'll leave us be?"

Elkman gives McGredy a sidelong glance. "Dunno why they'd appreciate us dumpin' our garbage on 'em…"

McGredy shrugs. "Jest a thought is all."

"Well, keep thinkin'…"

"You have a plan?"

"We eat some grub and move on."

"Yeah, and what about them?"

"They can feed themselves well 'nough."

The gambler surveys the area to see if there are more. "No, dammit! What are *we* going to do about *them*?"

"That's up to them, not us."

They both look over, as Amy slowly wakes and sits up. She startles at the sight of the Indians watching from the hill. Turning to meet the gaze of her companions, she gestures toward the riders. "What do we do about that?"

McGredy watches Elkman take another bite of biscuit. The gambler gets to his feet, walks past Amy and grumbles, "*They* don't mind, so not a damn thing apparently…"

Amy looks at Elkman, still chewing, and asks, "Tomas?"

"Git somethin' to eat, and we'll be on our way."

Chapter 32

The group travels east toward the mountains on the horizon. Elkman, with Amy beside him, leads, while Snarel, McGredy and Dobkins bring up the rear. From a distance, the pair of native riders shadow their back-trail. McGredy cranes his neck to check if they're still there. "Damnation… They sure know how t'make a man nervous."

The tracker nods and rides on without looking back. "Yessir… Dem bein' dere do take d'starch outta ya."

McGredy gestures to the gun that Snarel is leering at. "I'm gonna ride up t'see if our leader has a plan. If this feller does anythin' uncalled for, blast 'im."

Dobkins nods and eases a thumb over the two hammers. "Be my pleasure…"

McGredy catches the lead pair and rides between them. Elkman and Amy look at him and then back at the other two. Noticing that the natives are still on their trail, Elkman then turns to McGredy. "They're still following…" McGredy nods and Elkman adds, "How's that Dobkins fella workin' out?"

He glances back at the tracker holding the shotgun. "He's a good sort, I guess…" The gambler adjusts his coat lapel. "Still ain't certain if he's gonna blast me or not."

"*Most* folks feel that way 'bout *you*."

McGredy grimaces and turns to see Amy hiding a smile. He pivots back to Elkman. "I didn't come up here t'have my reputation tarnished in front of the lady."

Elkman adjusts his hat and nods to the gambler. "My apologies…"

Keeping pace with them, McGredy hooks a thumb over his shoulder. "What are we gonna *do* about 'em?"

"Who…?"

Exasperated, the gambler turns in his saddle and points directly at the two natives. "*Them…*"

Not turning to look, Elkman instead stares at something else ahead of them. "They may be the least of our worries."

McGredy utters, "How so…?" When he hears Amy let out a gasp, he turns forward. As a dozen Indian riders emerge from the surrounding hills McGredy chokes up on his horse's reins and hisses, "*Cripes…* The whole tribes comin' t'greet us." He looks at Elkman. "We gonna make a run fer it?"

Amy pivots in her saddle to look at the ones following, and then back again to the larger group heading their way. "Maybe they haven't seen us?"

Suddenly, a shrill, whooping war-call pierces the air. They all turn to gape at Bob Snarel, as he finishes the yell with a gleeful grin aimed toward his captors. Elkman turns forward, as the Indians respond to the outburst with their own cry and urge their mounts forward. "Aww, damn…"

Shocked at Snarel's audacity, Amy blurts, "Why did he do *that*?"

McGredy growls, "I'm gonna *kill* that bastard!"

In a moment, a swarm of leather-fringed riders, greatly outnumbering the smaller party, make a circle around them. Elkman stops and raises a hand in greeting. Alongside him, McGredy leans over and whispers, "Ya speak sheep-eater?"

"No, but we come peaceful, and we mean no harm."

McGredy pushes back in the seat of the saddle and scans the excited crowd of native horsemen. "You and I know that, but how ya gonna let *them* know?"

Elkman clears his throat and loudly addresses the swarm of riders in simple English. "*We mean no harm…*"

Flabbergasted, McGredy turns to gawk at Elkman. "Uhh, hey pard, yer native dialect ain't too impressive…"

Behind them, Snarel raises his bound hands in the air and calls out in an unfamiliar tongue. The natives instantly halt to listen, while Elkman's group turns to face their captive. McGredy grumbles, "What's that durn bandit up to *now?*"

Reading the body language, Elkman senses the natives' receptive reaction. "Appears t'be none too good for us."

Dobkins eases his horse closer to Snarel and jabs his shotgun into the man's ribs. The captive keeps his hands raised, points at the black man and speaks in Northern Cheyenne. *"This warrior, with skin like night, is one of them, and he will kill and eat all of your womenfolk."*

Dobkins, flashing a knowing smile at Snarel, asks drolly, "Did ya say, *eat* yer women?"

Surprised, Snarel lowers his hands to stare at the scout. "Ya understood what I jest said?"

"Mostly."

Snarel looks disappointed. "Well, I guess I kin figger where ya learned yer trackin' skills."

Keeping the shotgun barrels pressed into Snarel's ribs, Dobkins clicks back the hammers and looks out at the Indians. "It sure warn't from *white* folk."

Chapter 33

Encircled by the Indians, the group clusters together. McGredy watches as the pair that were following them join the others and then speak to their leader. He turns to the scout. "Dobkins, if ya know their tongue, ya best say somethin' nice t'keep this meetin' friendly."

The tracker rests his shotgun across the pommel of his saddle and raises both hands in the air. He speaks loud and clear in a local Ute dialect, and the natives seem to understand. Snarel eyes the gun and makes a lunge for it. Quick as lightning, Dobkins takes hold of Snarel and pulls him from the saddle, over the horse's neck and to the ground.

The captive picks himself up and then looks at the dark-skinned tracker holding the shotgun on him. "Yer a quick one, arn't ya. I'll remember ta kill ya the first chance

I git." Unbothered, Dobkins cradles the gun on his arm, raises a hand, and addresses the Indians again. They understand his meaning, and some nod their consent.

Their leader advances for an exchange with Dobkins. After they finish, a few of the native riders start off to the north. Watching them go, McGredy asks, "What did he say, 'nd where are they goin'?"

"We will go to his village."

Elkman shifts in his saddle and looks at his companions. "Was he *askin'* or *tellin'?*"

Dobkins moves his horse, so Snarel can pass to mount. Then, with a serious look, he offers, "That was the chief's son. He said we will go to his village, and there they will decide what t'do with us."

Jefferson looks around. "No talkin' him out of it?"

"They find it uncommon to tie up a man that can speak their language, and…"

McGredy senses the tracker's hesitation. "And, what…?"

"The woman…"

Amy pipes in. "What about me?"

"They think ya will be a good wife."

She looks at the warriors and then turns back to Dobkins. "That may be, but not for one of *them*."

The tracker shrugs. "That's fer the chief to decide."

Elkman exchanges a look with Amy, and then looks at McGredy, who seems none too concerned about Amy's future. "What's *yer* take on this, McGredy?"

"I dunno… She's not *my* woman. Indians like to gamble, so maybe we can *win* her back."

Amy shakes her head. "*Gamble* for me...? Don't you *dare* leave me with them."

One of the warriors reaches over to cut the ties on Snarel's hands. With a quick glance at the others, Snarel grins, then spurs his horse and rides along with the departing Indians. Clenching his jaw at the sight of his prisoner riding free, Elkman mutters, "I guess we'll see what happens."

~*~

The natives usher the reluctant group of riders into a village mostly populated by older woman and small children. Despite the air of poverty, an atmosphere of contentment exists. After having been forewarned about the expected visitors, females of marrying age hide themselves away.

As the villagers line up to watch them enter the camp, the children, curious to see if they are real, reach out to touch. One of the kids pokes McGredy's leg with a carved stick, and the gambler digs into his vest pocket to pull out a shiny coin. After flashing it to the crowd of eager youngsters, he flips it toward them.

A mass of hands grab at the coin, until one of the larger boys smiles and displays his prize. McGredy eases his horse up next to Elkman. "See, I told ya. Ever'one likes to be a winner..."

The mob of children following McGredy hope for another act of generosity and Elkman looks behind then grins. "Looks like you've made some new friends."

"Ya say that like it don't happen often."

"Jest not 'xactly what I've seen happen in saloons..."

"When outta my element, I like t'keep it friendly..."

As they ride through the crowd, a few horseback warriors split off to monitor them. While following the chief's son toward the dwelling at the center of the village, Elkman notices that some of the braves have their eyes fixed on Amy as she rides past. He leans over to her. "You have admirers." Uneasy, she scans the attentive faces of the young warriors. Elkman continues, "Whatever ya do, don't show signs of fear, or you'll lose what power ya have over 'em."

Jokingly, McGredy pipes in. "If they get the notion yer not worthy, you'll be doin' squaw work like chewin' rawhide and sewin' buffalo skins."

She sits up straighter in the saddle and lifts her chin. "Jefferson, I'll see *you* doing that sort of work before *I* do."

McGredy smiles at her, then glances back at his own stream of admirers. "That's the attitude, l'il lady... Jest be *you*." As the group rides on, Dobkins positions himself at the rear, where he can keep a watchful eye on everyone.

Chapter 34

The group stops at the chief's dwelling, and the mounted warriors surround the visitors. While they wait for the chief to appear, one of the warriors gestures for them to dismount. Dobkins understands the need to show respect, and he is the first to step down, followed by the rest. Snarel continues to look for an opportunity to escape, and Dobkins, with the shotgun, moves up beside him to discourage his departure.

Finally, the Indian leader emerges to stand before them. With age-worn eyes, he analyzes the people presented to him. As he assesses each visitor, a warrior to his right leans in to whisper in a low tone. After the events that led them to the village are explained, the chief nods. His penetrating gaze lingers momentarily on Amy, and then the chief looks to Snarel. He utters a few words but receives no answer. The chief repeats himself to Dobkins, and he receives a curt answer in reply. Curious, Elkman asks, "What did he say?"

"He wants t'know this man's crime."

Elkman looks at Snarel, who chooses to remain silent. "Tell the chief that we aim to serve white man's law on him for acts of murder and theft."

Dobkins translates Elkman's words as best he can in Ute. The chief understands and nods. Snarel eyes the uneasy crowd, sensing that the situation is not in his favor.

Then, with interest, the chief eyes Amy. He utters a few words to the man next to him, and then addresses Dobkins. Amy turns to Elkman and asks, "What is he saying *now?*"

Before Elkman can respond to her, Dobkins answers. "No disrespect intended, but it's best if womenfolk left things unsaid, so they don't git the wrong impression."

Not liking to be hushed, she addresses Elkman directly. "*Really…?* And, what impression is *that?*"

Elkman gives her a sly wink, and then barks at her. "*Quiet, woman!* Speak only when spoken to."

As Amy's eyes go wide with disbelief, McGredy grins, enjoying the spectacle. Glaring at Elkman, she clenches her jaw in contempt and stands straighter. Elkman turns to the leader, offers a nod, and then looks to Dobkins. "What did he say?"

"He would like t'marry her t'one of his warriors."

"Which one…?"

Amy stomps her foot, and before she can speak up, Elkman chides her. *"Behave, woman!!!"* He raises an open hand as if to strike, and she backs down, taking part in the charade. The onlookers praise his strict response and nod with approval. When all is quiet, the chief speaks to the scout and then gestures toward a group of young bucks.

Dobkins nods his understanding and turns to Elkman. "They are to compete for her."

Elkman glances at Amy and then studies the warriors. "Tell the chief and his people that we are honored by this offer, but we must decline. The woman is promised to another."

Amy starts to say something, and Elkman shushes her. Dobkins relays the message, and the chief steps up to them. Staring right at Elkman, the chief speaks as Dobkins translates. *"Who is this woman promised to?"*

Without breaking eye contact with the Indian leader, Elkman responds. "Tell them that this woman is to marry *me."*

Shocked at the unexpected turn of events, McGredy and Amy blurt out in unison. *"What…?!?"*

Elkman turns to look at them. "What…?"

Dobkins translates Elkman's response, and the chief stands stone-faced a while. Finally, he cracks a grin and speaks. Dobkins shares, *"If you choose to keep this woman for yourself, then you must compete with one who has challenged your ownership."* Satisfied with the proposal, the chief raises his hands and addresses those surrounding them.

When the chief is done speaking, he steps back inside his dwelling. Elkman turns to Dobkins, and the tracker explains, "Tomorrow, there'll be a show of arms t'compete fer the ownership of this woman."

Elkman grimaces. "What *kind* of show?"

"You'll have t'fight one of these braves."

"I don't want to hurt anyone."

As the crowd disperses, Dobkins looks around and then looks back to Elkman and the others. "Ya jest have ta win… And, not git yerself kilt."

Chapter 35

Inside one of the wickiups, Elkman, McGredy and Dobkins sit, across from Snarel, on blankets and assorted animal hides. Elkman watches outside, as Amy is led to another lodge where a group of women are gathered around. He turns to Dobkins. "What're they gonna to do with her?"

"They are t'prepare her t'accept matrimony."

"With whoever survives tomorrow's affair…?"

Dobkins nods. "I'm 'fraid so… That's the way it works."

McGredy chuckles. "Ya really got yerself set up good. Looks to be, yer fightin' ta git hitched."

Exhausted, Elkman lowers his gaze and heaves a sigh. "Always been t'other way with me…"

The gambler offers, "Could slip out in the night."

Rubbing his tired eyes, Elkman mutters thoughtfully. "N'er been in a situation t'fight for a woman b'fore."

While studying their temporary accommodations, McGredy asks, "What's changed?"

Irritated to see Snarel smugly sitting across from them, Elkman scratches his cheek and looks for a place to bed down. "Lack of sleep might have somethin' to do with it."

Noticing that he is still under Dobkin's watchful eye, Snarel reclines where he is. He sees McGredy get to his feet to pace the interior of the small space. The gambler stops and stares when Elkman lies down and places a hat over his face. "Ya cain't sleep at a time like this."

"Can't I…?"

"Ya ain't concerned 'bout what ya signed up fer?"

"I'm jest tired…"

"What 'bout what comes after?"

Elkman adjusts the brim of his hat and settles in to get some sleep. "Either I'll be dead, or married."

McGredy's jaw drops in disbelief. Gawking at Elkman, he states, "In *my* book, it's the *same damn thing.*"

Elkman murmurs, "Wake me when the doin's begin."

As Dobkins settles in to guard Snarel, the astonished gambler watches Elkman quickly drift off to sleep. Finally, McGredy turns to Dobkins and gestures toward the prisoner. "I'll watch 'im. This idea of wedlock has me too riled to rest."

Grateful for the respite, the tracker passes his shotgun to McGredy and lays back to sleep. In a moment, both Elkman and Dobkins are snoring, and McGredy sits to face Snarel. Sneering, the outlaw grumbles, "Too bad it ain't *you* that's t'git hitched."

McGredy points the gun at him. "Why's that…?"

"Save me the trouble of killin' ya."

"Ya think I wouldn't win out?"

Snarel puts his hands behind his head and answers. "Between *them* choices, there ain't *no* winner…"

~*~

Later that evening, blazing campfires light up the night. There is big excitement in the air due to the coming event. Looking outside through the doorway, McGredy sits with the shotgun pointed at Snarel. Dobkins wakes and notices that Elkman is still sleeping. He asks the gambler, "All is well?"

"So far… They've jest bin settin' up fer a party."

"It's big doin's…"

"The fight or the matrimony…?"

The tracker sits up and wipes sleep from his eyes. "Fightin' is a way of life here. They pride themselves on their skills with weapons 'n womenfolk."

Overhearing, Elkman stirs and lifts his hat from his face. "Sounds like McGredy's behavior at a card table."

McGredy mutters, "Hey pard, now that yer rested some, maybe you'll reconsider the challenge?"

"The fight or the marriage…?"

"One 'n the same to me…"

Sitting up, Elkman smoothes his hair and puts on his hat. "Figure if I lose the fight, I won't have t'worry 'bout the other."

"At least there's a bright side."

Elkman turns to Dobkins. "You ever seen one of these nuptial challenges b'fore?"

Dobkins glances at the shotgun in McGredy's lap and then to Snarel, who is listening. Turning back to Elkman, Dobkins answers, "I lived with a northern tribe after the war."

Elkman glances at the pistol wrapped up in his gun rig. "Why'd they let us keep our weapons?"

"They have the woman... We're free ta go anytime, if'n we leave her b'hind as a gift."

McGredy lights up with excitement. "Problem solved...! Why the hell didn't ya say that b'fore?"

Elkman shoots him a glare, then peers out to one of the bonfires. As he pulls his gun rig to his lap, Dobkins states, "You'll have no need fer dat shooter. It'll be hand t'hand. Knives 'r clubs."

Tilting his head, McGredy offers, "I'd choose the clubs. How hard can it be t'swing one?"

Dobkins eyes McGredy. "Clubs is da worst. It ain't da swingin' part that's hard, but not gittin' whacked."

McGredy tries to be helpful. "Well, if ya get thumped, I'd imagine it'd be over pretty quick."

"It is, at that."

Elkman doesn't enjoy the thought of having his head bashed and wonders aloud. "Whose choice'll it be?"

Dobkins grimaces. "T'ain't yourn. Usually it's da choice of the challenger." As they all look at the fires glowing outside, they sense increased activity in anticipation of the big contest. The tracker asks, "How are ya wit' a knife?"

"Fair to middlin'…"

McGredy proposes, "Maybe they'll choose fist-tacuffs. I've seen Elkman in a bar fight, and he can hold his own."

Elkman scoffs at the notion. "Any fight *you* was 'round, I was holdin' up *yer end* of it."

"No need to be snippy with me… I was jest tryin' to give ya some encouragement."

Then a warrior appears at the doorway and casts his shadow over the room. Addressing them, Dobkins translates. "It is time…"

McGredy exchanges a look of trepidation with Elkman. Then, he shrugs dolefully, as he watches him get up and stretch. Climbing to his feet, the gambler points the shotgun at Snarel to usher him to the door. "C'mon… Git up. Time t'go."

As Snarel starts to stand, the warrior in the doorway looks their way, points, and gives a command.

Elkman looks to Dobkins. "What'd he say?"

"He stays."

McGredy glances around at the others, and then back to Snarel before protesting. "The *hell* he does! This slippery coyote will b'gone lickety-split, if'n he ain't watched."

Unmoved, the warrior stares at them, while Dobkins does his best to translate McGredy's concerns. Finally, understanding the problem, the warrior brings in the teenager who caught the coin earlier. Dobkins exchanges words with the warrior and then states. "He will watch."

McGredy warily eyes the youth and then looks at Snarel before turning back to Dobkins. "Ask him how he'll be able t'keep this man from leavin'?"

The tracker utters a few words, and the boy produces a small bow with several arrows. Unsure, Dobkins suggests, "Maybe we should leave him da shotgun?"

McGredy shakes his head. "I'd rather not have it handy fer Snarel t'git his hands on."

When the warrior waves them all outside, McGredy reluctantly complies. On his way out, he winks at the youth, flips him another coin, and then points at Snarel. "If'n he moves from that spot, you shoot 'im with one of them pointed sticks. Two or three, if need be…" He then looks to Dobkins, and the tracker translates what was said.

As they leave, Snarel smugly smiles and gives a wave. "Bye, now fellas… Enjoy the show." He lies back comfortably, as the others proceed to the festivity. With a glimmer in his eye, he notices that Elkman has left his holstered pistol behind.

Chapter 36

Blazing bonfires illuminate an open area in the middle of the Indian camp. Elkman and his party are ushered to one side of the fighting circle, and the warriors gather opposite them. McGredy scans the eager faces and shakes his head. "Don't imag'n too many'll be cheerin' fer you."

Elkman studies the crowd. "Where's Amy?"

As if on cue, Amy is brought to the arena. She is dressed in a beaded, buckskin outfit, with flowers braided into her hair. As she sits at the chief's side, the sight of her silences the crowd.

McGredy scratches his beard and glances at Elkman. "Dang, she's somethin' purty." Elkman gives him a stern look. The gambler shrugs and adds, "Well, at least that gives ya a little motivation ta help ya try ta win."

Elkman looks across the circle to the group of warriors, trying to figure out which one he will have to battle. "Yeah… Sure gives the other fella somethin' to fight for, too."

McGredy tugs at his beard and nods. "Yeah, the sight of her does get the blood to rise."

Elkman glances back at McGredy again and grimaces. "Jefferson, ya ain't helpin' none…"

The gambler slaps him on the back. "Good luck."

Across the circle, the warriors step aside, and a tall, well-muscled young man moves forward. Dobkins whispers, "That's who yer fightin'."

Worried, McGredy considers Elkman's odds. "Damn… That's some *bad* luck."

Elkman takes a breath and asks, "What is…?"

"I was hopin', for yer sake, that it would be one of the older fellas. Or, at least maybe a smaller one…"

"Why…?"

"That young buck is nimble 'nd eager t'git a wife."

Stretching, Elkman mutters, "I'm quick 'nough…"

With a less than reassuring smile, the gambler eyes the grey in Elkman's whiskers. "*Sure* ya were. Twenty years ago…"

Across the way, the young man takes off his decorated breastplate, and the other braves rub animal grease on his bare arms and chest. His sinewy muscles gleam in the firelight. Elkman hands his hat to McGredy and unbuttons his vest. Around them, the crowd begins to chant and dance. McGredy, seeing that the brave's side is encouraging the competition, turns to Elkman. "Ya want me t'rub grease on ya?"

Elkman removes his vest and then pulls off his shirt. "Jest hold my stuff..." With his stark, white chest vivid in the firelight, he steps into the ring. The warrior breaks from his friends and approaches. Elkman glances at Amy, seated next to the chief, and bows his head. With a forced smile, she doesn't look too reassuring.

Both combatants are brought to the middle of the arena, and the challenger is presented with his choice of weapons. Poised, the warrior waves the clubs away and chooses knives. Elkman is given a stag-handled blade, and he weighs it in hand. He stares at his opponent, assessing his strength while searching for any apparent weakness. The warrior has a deadly look on his face, as Elkman reluctantly takes a fighting stance. "I don't wanna hurt ya, kid..."

The young brave lunges at him, and the fight is on. Elkman leaps to the side and swipes. Steel clashes when the warrior hits Elkman's blade with his own. The fighters circle, probing each other's defense with quick jabs.

From the sideline, McGredy cups his hands around his mouth and hollers, "Don't git close, or he'll stick ya fer sure!" Briefly thinking about Snarel, McGredy looks over at the dwelling where they were kept. His gaze connects with Dobkins, and he leans over to whisper. "If Tomas don't survive, what's ta happen with *us?*"

"If'n we don't wanna try 'n git the woman fer ourselves, the best choice is t'leave quick."

Turning back to the fight, they see Elkman defending himself against the able-bodied warrior. With a frown, McGredy protests, "We cain't leave her to some eager pup."

"Then, *you'll* have t'fight t'marry her."

Concerned, McGredy turns his focus back to the match. "C'mon, Elkman…! Git in there close!!!"

Chapter 37

As the fires are fed with more wood to bring the blazes higher, the fighters circle and jab at each other. Drenched with sweat, they continue to thrust and parry with flashing steel blades. When one of the warrior's lunges slices across Elkman's ribs, he quickly swings out to crash his knuckles into the brave's jaw. The unexpected blow rattles the warrior, but he quickly rallies when he sees the streak of blood on his opponent's side.

Elkman, still swift on the defensive, is starting to fatigue. The warrior's gleaming body drips with sweat and animal grease as he continually jabs and lunges. Elkman brandishes his knife in front of him, blocking the brave's blows. The shiny steel flashes back and forth in the firelight.

Observing the frenzied crowd, McGredy realizes that the match is not going in Elkman's favor. He yells above the vociferous cheers. "Git in close, or he'll carve ya ta pieces!" Elkman blocks as best he can, but some of the stabbing blows make contact, slicing his arms and torso.

The natives chant encouragement, and the brave redoubles his efforts. Empowered by the yelling, the warrior hastily lunges in, and Elkman counters by charging forward. With a smack, the sweaty, blood-streaked bodies slam together. Elkman rakes his blade across the man's shoulders and locks his other arm around the warrior's knife hand. Dirt cakes their bodies in muddy streaks, as they tumble to the ground. Screaming cheers erupt from the crowd, as the two men whip themselves into a frenzy of bloodlust. In close combat, they roll across the arena, each attempting to avoid getting stuck by the other's probing blade.

Distressed, Amy stands clutching her arms across her chest. She looks at McGredy, who glances back to where Snarel is being kept and then turns back to the fighting. He hollers, "Better finish it quick, or he'll wear ya down!"

As the combatants roll across the ground, it is hard to distinguish one mud-caked man from the other. Eventually, Elkman gets the upper hand and delivers several hard blows. One knife drops and Elkman gets up with his still in hand, kicking the other aside.

From the sidelines, McGredy frantically yells, "Dammit…! *Don't let 'im up!*"

Elkman takes a step back to allow his opponent to rise, and they both look at the dropped blade. As the undeterred warrior moves to it, Elkman, waving his knife, blocks him. "Let's end this b'fore someone gits hurt."

Looking back to his friends screaming encouragement, the warrior then marches over to the battle clubs. He picks one up and brazenly swings it around while advancing toward Elkman. Knife in hand, Elkman glances over toward McGredy.

Shocked, McGredy turns to Dobkins. "What the hell…? Can he *do* that?!"

The tracker shrugs. "It's their fight, so I guess they can do whate'er they want."

As the brave continues his advance, Elkman holds the knife blade out in front of him, warning, "We can stop this now and end it here peaceably..."

With a smiling nod, the warrior raises the club over his head and swings it at Elkman. Dodging the blow, Elkman ducks aside and thrusts his blade. Then, with surprising speed, the club comes around again and smacks Elkman's hand, knocking the knife free. The blade hits the ground, and his opponent is quick to move in front of where it landed.

As the warrior advances, Elkman clutches his injured hand and backs away. At the sidelines, McGredy asks Dobkins, "What can he do 'gainst that thing?"

"Not git hit…"

The warrior continues to make a show of swinging the club, as Elkman keeps out of his reach. He lunges in at the warrior and, with a *thwack* of the wooden bat, is knocked away. Elkman clutches his hurt shoulder, feeling for anything broken. He glances at McGredy, who turns his palms up and shrugs. On the attack again, the warrior cracks Elkman across the thigh and tumbles him to the ground. Elkman quickly rolls away to avoid another blow, as the business end of the club comes down hard on the ground.

Exhausted, Elkman gasps for air and climbs to his feet. He faces the advancing warrior, as his opponent performs another elaborate display of swinging the club. While the crowd chants at a fevered pitch, the young warrior stops to shout a final battle cry.

McGredy covers his eyes and turns away. "I can't look… Tell me when it's over." As the tracker keeps his full attention on the contest, the gambler trepidatiously turns back and peeks through his fingers.

Chapter 38

The warrior screams at the top of his lungs as he continues his assault on Elkman while twirling the battle club over his head. The distance closes, as Elkman moves back against the crowd with no room for retreat. With an intense war cry the warrior lifts the club higher.

As Elkman is pushed back against the sidelines, he produces one of the dropped knives retrieved from the ground. In one quick movement, he flicks his wrist to toss the blade at his opponent. The knife buries itself in the warrior's chest with a resounding *thunk,* as if sticking into the trunk of a tree.

With a look of surprise, the warrior releases his grip on the war club, and it goes sailing into the crowd of bystanders. Arms still raised, the warrior looks down at the knife buried hilt-deep in his torso. Turning to the crowd, he meets their stares of astonishment. Uttering quiet words under his breath, he stumbles toward them before falling to the ground in shock. Several braves lift and carry him away.

With mud and blood caking his body, Elkman stands, trying to catch his breath, while the crowd buzzes in disbelief. As McGredy and Dobkins step up to prevent him from falling, he rolls his head to the side to ask, "Did someone win?"

McGredy holds his arm to keep him on his feet. "Yeah… I think *you* did, pard."

"What happens now?"

The gambler scans the concerned villagers and then looks at Dobkins before responding. "We're about to find out." The crowd moves in to form a circle around Elkman's party, and the chief steps to the forefront. In a booming voice, for all to hear, he addresses them. McGredy whispers to Dobkins. "What's he sayin'?"

The tracker interprets. "He says that it was a good fight, and the contestants showed bravery. Especially, *our* man here."

McGredy looks at the bleeding wound on Elkman's ribs. "He *nearly* showed a lotta *guts*…"

As the chief continues with his speech, the crowd splits, and Amy is brought forward. Dobkins pauses, then translates. "He says the white warrior has earned the hand of this woman, and she will serve and care for 'im until she is dead or..."

McGredy hisses, "Or what…?"

"*Sold,* I think…"

Amy stares at Elkman, and tears streak down her face at the sight of his mud-caked wounds. McGredy tilts his head and whispers to Dobkins. "What're we s'posed t'do now?"

"Not sure, but I think he's marryin' them now."

The chief raises his arms to the heavens, then he takes Amy by the hand and leads her forward to join her husband. Looking at each other, the couple can't help but smile at their contrasting appearances. McGredy and Dobkins step back, leaving Elkman to stand on his own in front of Amy. Touched, the gambler sniffs. "Is he officially hitched?"

As the chief finishes, Dobkins turns. "It 'pears so."

Hand in hand, Elkman and Amy are ushered back to where Amy was prepped for the event. Dobkins, noticing McGredy rubbing an eye, frankly asks, "Are ya cryin'?"

"Heck, no…! But, I *should* be… Sad t'see a good man git hisself into somethin' like that."

"You ain't n'er bin hitched?"

McGredy puffs his chest and slips his hand into his vest. "Some've tried, but none succeeded."

Dobkins lowers his gaze to reflect. "Seems a lifetime ago, but I had me a wife and kid before, back when I was a slave."

"Where are they now?"

"As the war was near upon us, I was sold off, and I n'er could find 'em after that." They remain silently somber, as they watch the crowd disperse and the fires slowly diminish.

~*~

The flap-door of the wickiup swings closed, and Elkman stands in the light of a fire burning in the center of the room. Amy stares at him. Finally, he breaks the silence. "I'm sorry..."

"For what...?"

"This whole thing... I dunno, 'xactly."

Uncertain of how to respond, she continues to stare. When Elkman looks down at his mud-streaked lacerations and touches one of them with his dirty fingers, she stops him. "Don't do that."

He peers at her, as she studies his multiple injuries. "What're ya thinkin' I should do?"

"You're a mess. I'm trying to figure out where to start."

She moves him over to a bearskin rug and then picks up the bowl of water and wash cloth that was set by the doorway. Tired, he gingerly sits and stares up at her. "Uh... I wasn't sure how that was gonna end."

Amy squeezes the rag and wipes at one of his wounds. Clenching his jaw, he winces, then murmurs softly. "But... When I saw ya lookin' like that..." She finishes cleaning one of his cuts and dips the cloth to rinse it. The pain is terrible and, to keep from fainting, Elkman takes a deep breath. He mumbles, "With all that we havta deal with, this was *not* on my list..." She meets his dazed look and continues to clean him up. Confused as to what she might be thinking, he babbles, "I, uh... Why aren't ya sayin' anythin'?"

She looks down to wash out the rag, squeezes it, and then begins to wash him again, murmuring, "A wife should be a good listener to her husband."

Surprised at her diplomatic tone, he relaxes at her touch. "So, we're really married then…?"

"Yes, for now… In *this* place, we are." She rinses the cloth in the basin and washes his torso.

"I might as well enjoy it while it lasts."

"Enjoy what…?"

"*You* not havin' much t'*say*…"

She dabs his wound a little less gently, and he winces. With a curt smile, she proposes, "Once I have you all fixed up, I'll have *plenty* to say."

He looks down at the caring hands on his bare chest. "I'm in no position to argue."

Wiping the washrag over his battered body, she nods. "No, Tomas Elkman, you are not."

Chapter 39

McGredy and Dobkins stumble drunkenly to their dwelling, while sharing from a hollowed-out gourd. The inebriated pair bump into each other as they attempt to enter. McGredy steps aside and Dobkins pulls back the blanket covering the entrance, stopping short as he peers inside.

Sprawled at their feet is the Indian boy who was left behind to guard Snarel. His head twisted in an unnatural way, there is an arrow buried deep in his chest. Just below the arrow is the coin that the gambler had tossed the youth earlier. Swallowing hard, McGredy mutters, *"Damn..."*

Dobkins drops the nearly empty gourd and turns to look out past the camp into the darkness. "He's gone far from here, 'nd we won't be able t'follow 'til mornin'."

McGredy steps inside to survey the shelter. He notices Elkman's empty holster, and that the youth's bow is broken, only connected by the sinew cord. He turns to the tracker. "Dobkins, yer under no obligation t'me, but I'll be goin' after 'im at first light. Yer trackin' skills would be highly welcome."

The scout looks down at the boy and shakes his head. "When da devil is on the loose, it's a man's duty ta put 'im down."

~*~

Amy has cleaned Elkman's body and wrapped his cuts with bandages. He is stripped down to his under-britches, and they lie next to each other on the bearskin. Amy sits up and looks at him. "How long will we stay?"

"A few days is all."

"Where will we go…?" Reading his thoughts, she knows he is thinking about Snarel. "After, I mean…"

He gingerly raises his arm to scratch the back of his head. "I ain't put much thought to it."

"My uncle's ranch would be a good place to start."

"It's a fine spread."

They are quiet for a moment, while she gently touches her hand over his bandages. "My father needs to be told."

His gaze moves to meet hers. "About yer uncle?"

She sits up further and stares down at him in disbelief. "How soon you forget that we have been wed!"

"I ain't forgot."

She smiles and starts to peel off her deerskin outfit. Slowly, the leather falls off her arm. "I can help you remember." Elkman winces in pain, as he shifts to give her room to stand. After disrobing, she kneels next to him and pulls up a blanket. With a gentle touch, she smooths a lock of hair on his forehead and then gives him a kiss.

Amy settles in close and wraps the blanket around them. She hears heavy breathing, and notices that he has fallen asleep. Disappointed, she touches her fingers across his bruised cheek, scoots closer and whispers in his ear. "Tomas… I'll remind you again tomorrow."

~*~

At daybreak, McGredy and Dobkins mount up and prepare to leave. They look over at Elkman's honeymoon abode. The tracker chews his bottom lip and wonders aloud. "Shouldn't we let 'im know?"

The gambler checks his rifle and then shakes his head. "He's got other business to attend."

Dobkins smiles and turns his horse away from the camp. "He'll be some angry with ya."

McGredy nods and thinks on the course they're taking. "Sure will… If it's not one thing, it's another."

The tracker eases his horse up alongside McGredy's. "The way ya talk… Ya sure *you* ain't bin hitched?"

"Why…?"

"Ya sure sound as if ya had a woman at home who bin naggin' yer hide fer some time."

The gambler stares out beyond the camp. "I ain't sayin' they n'er got close. Jest that I n'er had the rope slip tight…" McGredy points north. "We follow his tracks that a'way?"

Dobkins gathers the reins between his fingers and nods. "Yassir, I talked with some 'ere who say there's a minin' camp jest to the north, called Sawtooth City."

The mention of a likely town peaks McGredy's interest. "If there're rough folks 'round, that's where he's headed." McGredy looks at Dobkins who sits with the shotgun cradled across his lap. "My bet is that he's hopin' t'meet up with a posse that could be after us, as well."

Dobkins sighs. "Like as not, he'll round one up."

"Unless we find 'im first, 'nd drape 'im o'er a saddle." Without reply, the tracker nudges his horse and trots on. Sullenly, McGredy spurs his horse and follows after Dobkins, leaving the Indian village behind.

Chapter 40

With a buckskin hide draped over his naked shoulders, Elkman steps from the wickiup. The morning sun brings warmth to his body, and he breathes in a lungful of fresh air. His wounds are bandaged, and most of the dirt has been shaken from his pants. Noticing that people are gathering near the shelter he was held in before the contest, he walks over.

As he approaches the crowd, he hears whimpering cries from a woman inside. He moves past the ones at the entrance and looks in to see several women kneeling by a boy being prepared for burial. Noticing that McGredy and the others are not present, he asks, "What's happened?"

They turn to meet his gaze with mournful stares. Scanning the dwelling, he sees his bedroll, where his shirt, vest, and hat have been placed. He is surprised to find the holster on his gunbelt empty, and that all his companions' gear is gone. The women resume their chores, offering ceremonial burial chants and wails of sorrow to guide the spirit of the deceased into the afterlife.

Gingerly, Elkman shrugs off the deer hide and goes to grab his clothes. Under his shirt, he finds a note from McGredy. The scribbled message reads: *Bob killed that boy. We are on his trail and will do the same for him.*

Elkman recognizes the teenager from when they first entered the camp. He puts on his vest, fastens the buttons and then reaches to grab his hat. Looking around, he finds his rifle scabbard empty and assumes that Snarel has taken that as well. As Elkman gathers the rest of his gear, Amy stops at the entry. He turns when he hears her ask, "Where are you going?"

"Our ol' pal has done 'nother terrible deed in the night, 'nd they have gone after him."

"When did they leave?"

"First light, I imagine…"

Skeptical, she stares at him and then the empty scabbard. "You expect to find them?"

Elkman rolls his blanket and ties it. "I do."

"What about me?"

"Stay here, 'til I return."

Ever the strong-willed woman, she steps from the entry. "I'll get my things."

"No..."

Surprised at his response, she turns to her newly acquired husband. Facing her, Elkman musters the courage to declare, "I need ya to stay here. I jest fought to keep ya safe, 'nd I can't be doin' it again if I'm to find 'im."

Staring at him for a moment, she clenches her jaw, turns and walks away. Watching her leave, he refrains from calling her back. He is left sensing the weight of his actions as the women surrounding him continue to grieve.

~*~

Villagers silently observe Elkman, as he saddles his horse and loads his gear. In vain, he searches the crowd for Amy but doesn't see her. After glancing at his empty scabbard, he touches his hip, feeling for his missing sidearm. "Damn… Could use a gun." Turning to face the throng of ogling natives, he pantomimes. "Gun… I need a rifle. *Does anyone understand?*" The request is met by empty stares and a few responses in a language that he can't comprehend.

Finally, Elkman slips his boot into a stirrup and mounts. As he searches the crowd, he spots Amy coming forward. Holding her own rifle, she offers it up to him as she approaches. "I can't stop you, so take this."

He takes the gun. "I'll be back for you."

She watches him slide the rifle into his scabbard, and then she hands him a box of cartridges. As he leans back to slip the ammunition into his saddlebags, she declares, "Be careful… And, you come back to me."

Elkman tips his hat to her. "Will do…"

"You *promise* me, Tomas Elkman."

Their gaze locks, and he nods to her. "I promise…" Elkman gathers his reins, turns his mount and makes his way through the crowd. He prods his horse into a trot as he clears the village, and then he urges the animal to gallop.

Chapter 41

Elkman rides across flat prairie toward the mountains that span the horizon. Despite being on the hunt, he strikes a figure at peace with the world. Looking for tracks, he stops his horse, dismounts and squats to study the ground. His gaze lifts to scan the hills ahead, and he contemplates where the trail might lead.

Alone with his thoughts, Elkman takes out his tobacco pouch with rolling papers and reflects on the outlaw he seeks. After rolling a smoke, he lights a match and touches it to the cigarette before shaking out the flame. After tossing the match, he mounts and rides on.

~*~

The mining settlement of Sawtooth City earns its claim to be a boomtown. Dozens of patrons come and go from various crude establishments that include several bustling saloons. McGredy and Dobkins take in the activities, as they ride through town. When the gambler hears the snapping shuffle of a deck of cards, he gets a strong urge to stop and pull up a chair.

Dobkins glances over at the gambler. "Ya look jumpy... Ya gonna be okay?"

McGredy breaks his study of the gaming houses and pats his vest where his money usually resides. "Yeah... I'm fine. Where d'ya s'pose we'll find that fella?"

"He could be gittin' a drink somewheres, or he could be gatherin' up hired guns."

"Or both..."

Dobkins nods, as he looks around. "Check the stables, and I'll go beyond the edge of town t'see if he traveled on."

With surprise, the gambler turns to look at the tracker. "Really...? You can pick up a trail through *this?*"

The man nods. "Unless he switched his hoss."

At the livery, McGredy waves to Dobkins before splitting off. "You'll find me later...?"

"Yassir I'll find ya, like as not."

~*~

Elkman follows the horse trail toward the mountains. Momentarily, he stops his mount to scan the forested ridges. The telltale campfire smoke from a boomtown spreads and rises above the trees. He twists in the saddle to look behind, makes sure no one is following him, then rides on.

As he trots along, he reaches forward to pull Amy's rifle from the scabbard. He cocks the lever to chamber a round before casually laying the firearm across his lap. Elkman scans the path forward, as he mentally prepares himself for another encounter with Snarel.

~*~

Inside one of the many saloons of Sawtooth City, McGredy stands at the bar with a shot of whiskey. He eyes the room and sees a game table with an empty chair. He takes a sip, considers the players, and then glances at the front entrance. Seeing no sign of either Dobkins or Snarel, he grunts to himself. "Won't hurt anythin' to sit in on a few hands while I wait."

Moving over to the table, McGredy realizes that the only available seat would have his back to the door. After glancing back to the entrance, he asks, "Is this chair taken, gents?" Receiving a welcoming nod, he slides into the seat and pulls up to the game.

~*~

Late in the day the activity in the boomtown picks up. As the sun dips behind the mountains, lanterns are lit, and their glow illuminates the thoroughfare. Searching for McGredy, Dobkins peeks into establishments as he walks the boardwalk. He holds the shotgun down by his side and does his best to conceal it under his coat.

At the gaming table, McGredy grins at the other players, as he hauls in another pile of winnings. "My luck is holdin'…" The other cardplayers' faces suddenly turn grim, as someone steps up behind the gambler. When McGredy starts to turn, he hears the click of a pistol along with a familiar voice.

"Yer luck has jest run out."

McGredy stops handling his money and half-turns to see Snarel behind him with a gun pointed at the back of his head. He considers his chances, but the odds quickly diminish, when three more men step alongside Snarel. McGredy rests his hand on the table. "Bin lookin' fer ya."

Snarel grins. "Ya found me." With the barrel of the gun, he gestures for McGredy to stand. "Git up." The gambler starts to collect his winnings and Snarel shakes his head. "No, sir… Ya can leave that fer the table."

McGredy stares at the money, then turns to look at the gun and grumbles, "Who d'ya think ya are?"

Snarel nods to the men alongside him, and they lift their weapons to point at the gambler. "*I'm* the one with the *posse.*"

McGredy scoots his chair back and stands. He glances around the room and then looks toward the open doorway. Everyone in the room is watching, but no one intervenes. Taking note of McGredy's desire for a rescue, Snarel laughs. "Where's yer pal? Ya come here lookin' for me *alone?*"

Realizing that no one is coming to his aid, McGredy tucks a thumb into his vest. "Figured I'd run into ya sometime."

Pleased with himself, Snarel waves the barrel of his gun toward the door. "Yep… Ya found me, alright."

Resisting the urge to lunge at Snarel, the gambler starts to walk toward the door. "Where we goin'?"

"Not far…"

As McGredy nears the entrance, the bat-wing doors swing open, and Dobkins, with the double-barreled shotgun raised at hip level, steps inside. His eyes find the gambler, then travel to Snarel a few paces back. "Jest keep walkin', McGredy, 'nd ya others kin stay put."

The gambler quickens his pace, moving to the side to allow the tracker to get a clean shot with the scattergun. Dobkins pulls back both hammers and stares hard at the three men standing behind Snarel. "Ya's best git yer minds set right, or some folks could git themselves kilt."

The men glare at the business end of the shotgun and reluctantly lower the aim of their guns. With a thwarted shrug, Snarel lowers his own weapon and glances back at his men. "When there's one, there's usually another…" At an impasse, he addresses Dobkins and McGredy. "That other fella with ya? Or, did he not make it outta the fight?"

Dobkins ignores the question and glances at McGredy. "Our horses are outside."

The gambler protests. "What about *him?*"

The tracker turns his stare back to the well-armed posse. "This ain't the time…"

Snarel grins, as the men behind him step up and fan out. "No worries… We'll be along shortly."

One of the posse members lifts his gun and cocks it. "Hey, we ain't gonna let 'em *leave,* are we? I want my *money!*" He aims and fires, and the bullet cuts over McGredy's shoulder, smashing into the doorframe. Dobkins turns his shotgun and lets off one of the barrels. The blast booms through the barroom, and the man who fired his pistol tumbles back to the floor. Catching several pellets through his sleeve, Snarel jumps aside while firing his gun. Following suit, the others aim and fire.

McGredy touches the spot where the bullet grazed him and then, through the haze of gunsmoke, ducks out the door. Dobkins lets off the other barrel in Snarel's direction and backs up while cracking the gun open to reload. When another bullet whizzes by, McGredy grabs Dobkins by the coat and pulls him outside. *"Let's git the hell outta here!"*

Spotting their waiting mounts, McGredy hops from the boardwalk to land in his saddle. He sees the tracker plunk two fresh shells into the scattergun and then snap the breach closed. "How'd ya know t'bring the horses?"

Dobkins mounts up. "When I saw ya settin' at the table, I *figured* we'd need our horses to git out quick..."

With a quizzical look, McGredy asks, "You bin listenin' t'stories from Elkman?!?"

Dobkins gets himself situated in his saddle and lets off another shot toward the entryway to keep the men at bay. "No..." He pivots toward McGredy. "Ya done this b'fore?"

McGredy pulls his pistol and snaps a shot at the saloon. "Yeah... A few times..."

After firing the other barrel, Dobkins turns his horse and waves for them to leave. "No time fer wild stories. Let's git!" Through a hail of gunfire, the men race out of town.

Chapter 42

At the outskirts of town, Elkman stops his horse when he hears the pop of gunfire. Clenching his jaw, he peers ahead at the scrambling throng of bystanders filling the crowded street. His first thought escapes his lips, "McGredy…?

In a moment, there are two riders galloping toward him. The familiar pair reaches and continues past him. Elkman turns his horse and yells after them. "Jefferson… What's happened?"

Over his shoulder, the rabble-rousing gambler hollers, "Come on along, and we'll tell ya…!"

Glancing back at the town, Elkman can see several men mounting horses. He sinks spur and rides after the fleeing pair. Elkman gallops to catch up with them and looks behind to see others in pursuit. He yells to McGredy. "Who's that comin'?"

"Bob Snarel..."

"You found 'im?"

"He found *us*..."

"He's comin' after *you*?"

"Yep."

Still at a gallop, Elkman glances behind at the posse. "Who's that with 'im?"

"He bought some new pals. Not sure what's promised, but they're ready t'shoot first and ask questions later."

Dobkins pulls up beside them and adds, "We look t'be matched fer horses. They'll prob'ly run theirs down."

After a quick glance back to the town, Elkman turns to study the rolling terrain ahead, and points to a group of trees. "We can hold 'em off there at the timber." In agreement, they veer toward the stand of trees, as Snarel and his riders follow.

They reach the cover of the wooded area, clutching their firearms as they hop from their horses. The pursuing riders pop off a few shots as they get closer. Elkman levers Amy's rifle, snugs the gun against his shoulder and takes careful aim. McGredy squints toward the approaching riders. "If you can pick off that damn outlaw at this distance, it'll put a lot of our problems t'rest."

Elkman sights down the rifle barrel and waits for the posse to get nearer. Dobkins, behind him, not wanting to waste a shot at the out-of-range targets, holds a shotgun at the ready. Elkman steadies his aim until McGredy prods, "Dammit… Cain't ya hit 'im yet?"

His concentration broken, Elkman glances at McGredy. "I know *you* sure cain't."

Peering down at his gun, the gambler meekly shrugs. "Sittin' at a card table, I ain't often in need of rifle practice."

Elkman snorts, resumes his careful aim and then gently squeezes the trigger. The shot tags the rider to the left of Snarel, knocking the man off his horse.

McGredy claps Elkman on the back. "Good one, pard! Now, on the next shot, aim for Snarel."

Elkman frowns at McGredy, levers another cartridge into the chamber and snugs the rifle to his shoulder again. "That's who I was intendin' ta hit…" Elkman adjusts his aim, as the riders slow down.

McGredy leans over, breathing down Elkman's neck. "That's fine, pard… Hell, I figured ya was jest tryin' t'send a warnin' shot to them others."

"Will ya quit runnin' yer mouth…!" He squeezes off another shot, and one of the horses takes the bullet. "Damn…" Elkman lowers the rifle and levers it to cycle a fresh cartridge. When the riders halt, Elkman doesn't lift the gun to aim again.

McGredy eagerly points at them. "Take 'nother shot."

"I *don't* wanna hit 'nother *horse*."

"Why the hell *not?* Shoot 'em all 'nd put 'em afoot! Maybe, you'll git lucky and hit Bob yet."

Disappointed, Elkman gives McGredy a sour look. "What the hell happened in that town? How did he get those men gathered up so quick?"

McGredy glances over at Dobkins, who shakes his head as he turns away to tend to the horses. Turning back to Elkman, the gambler explains, "We tracked 'im to that town and had t'search 'im out."

Elkman looks at the tracker, then back to McGredy. "S'pose ya even had time for a quick game of cards?"

The gambler pats his vest where the remainder of his money is tucked. "Sometimes, the best way t'find someone is to quit lookin' 'nd wait fer 'em t'come to *you.*"

"Horseshit, McGredy…!"

"That's how I found *you* again."

"*You* were locked in *jail.*"

"Yeah, jest *waitin'* fer ya…"

Irritated with McGredy, Elkman turns to look at the posse that is holding back to maintain distance. He shakes his head in frustration and then heads off to tend to his horse. "We'll be at a standoff 'til nightfall."

Holding his rifle, McGredy looks to the distant group. "Dark… What then…?"

"Whatever they decide…"

Chapter 43

Elkman and his companions stare in the direction of the posse. In the far distance, a campfire flickers, but an accurate headcount can't be made. McGredy glances to where Elkman is leaning on a tree. "Whatcha thinkin'?"

Rifle held ready, Elkman peers into the dimness. "They'll send some of 'em out to ambush us."

McGredy gazes around. "I'd like us to sneak over there, git a' hold of 'im, and make an *end* to it."

"That's *one* of our options."

"What's the other?"

"Wait 'n see."

The gambler is silent for a moment and then whispers, "We could *leave*..."

"Then, we might not find 'im again to our advantage."

McGredy grunts, "Do we have the advantage?"

"Possibly…"

Dobkins comes up behind them and squats on his heels. "*I* could git at 'im, most likely."

They quietly exchange looks, until Elkman speaks. "What would we need t'do to help?"

"Trust me."

The gambler blurts, "That's *it…?*"

"And, stay here. As bait…"

McGredy nods. "Sounds like an *Elkman* plan."

"I know we's jest become acquainted, but they's gonna send some of 'em tonight, 'n Mista Snarel *will* be one of 'em." The tracker looks down at his shotgun. "If we're not sittin' here, they won't come. But, with you's both waitin' in the shadows, they won't know if it's only two or three of us."

Elkman nods. "We can hold here. When d'ya go?"

The tracker cradles the shotgun over his arm, stands and steps back into the darkness. "I's already gone…"

McGredy watches Dobkins quietly disappear by the horses and then looks at Elkman. "D'ya trust 'im?"

"If he's smart… He'll take his leave and be done with us."

The gambler scratches under his beard and then sighs. "*You* could've done that very thing, and jest stayed in the Indian village with yer new wife."

Elkman stares out toward the distant flickering campfire and nods. "Yeah… I said if he was *smart.*"

~*~

Later, Elkman and McGredy sit staring into the dark. Nearby, the horses shuffle their feet while fitfully dozing. Hearing a crunch on the dry grass, McGredy turns to listen.

"Tomas…"

"Yeah…"

In the silence, McGredy whispers, "Ya hear that?"

"Shh…" They squint into the darkness and see a man emerge from the shadows near the spot where they last saw Dobkins by the horses.

Softly, McGredy hisses, "O'er there…"

They watch and listen. Elkman cocks the hammer of his rifle which clicks exceptionally loud in the silence of the night. The ominous figure stops and turns toward the sound.

McGredy turns his gaze back to the far-off campfire. Then, when another dark figure passes between their position and the firelight, McGredy hollers, "Give 'em hell, boys…!!!" The muzzle of his rifle explodes with a flash of gunfire.

At the same time, Elkman catches a glimpse of the man creeping by their horses and fires. The simultaneous gunshots are met by several others, stabbing flames in their direction. Bullets whiz by, kicking up dirt and smashing into trees. Elkman levers his rifle, ducks, and dashes to another spot. "Keep movin', so they cain't draw a bead on ya!"

McGredy fires again, then scurries off into the darkness. Blasts of gunfire from all around light up the night. Elkman takes a shot and someone yelps in pain. Now near the horses, McGredy shoots his rifle again.

When the bullet slams against a rock, the man near it returns fire and then rushes the gambler. Knocked off his feet, McGredy tussles with his assailant.

Elkman returns fire, as shots flash around him. He spots his cohort near the horses and dashes in that direction. McGredy's attacker gets the upper hand and pulls out a pistol. As he aims it at the gambler, Elkman steps out of the shadows and smashes the butt of his rifle to the side of the man's head, knocking him out cold.

McGredy quickly gets to his feet and squints down at the laid-out man. "That warn't the one we want."

"I know..."

"Thanks, pard..."

"C'mon...! We're goin'." When the gambler grabs his rifle from the ground, he yelps as a bullet grazes his thigh. Elkman turns. *"You get hit?"*

"Jest barely..."

Quickly untying the horses, they mount and start firing blindly at any incoming flashes of gunfire. As they ride away, McGredy heads off in one direction, while Elkman strikes off in another. Cut adrift, Dobkins' saddled mount trails along.

Chapter 44

The next morning, Elkman rides, leading Dobkins' horse. Traveling through the empty campsite of the assailants, he watches and listens in case anyone is still around. As he passes by the smoldering remains of a fire, he looks to the distant stand of trees where the gunfight occurred the night prior.

Turning his gaze skyward, as he rides toward the wooded area, Elkman observes several birds circling overhead. Nearby, he investigates a body in the grass. When he doesn't recognize the man, he rides on. When he finally reaches the trees, he notices a figure seated on the ground.

His rifle perched on his thigh, ready, Elkman lets the lead rope to the trailing horse fall. "Hallo..." To his surprise, Bob Snarel turns to leer at him.

Shortly, Dobkins steps out from behind another tree, aiming the business end of his scattergun at the lone prisoner. As he tilts his hat back, he smiles at Elkman and announces, "Sure glad t'see ya."

Taking in the quiet surroundings, Elkman gazes around at the scattered shell casings on the ground. He notices another dead body in the grass where the horses were tied and then brings his attention back to Dobkins. "You's the only ones left?"

"He's the one I kept."

Elkman pivots to look behind. "I don't know where McGredy got to..."

"He ain't hereabouts..."

"I only caught *yer* horse."

"Fine by me if *this* fella walks." The tracker motions with the barrel of his gun, and Snarel gets up. He gestures toward Elkman, and ushers the prisoner onward.

Elkman can't help but feel uneasy in the man's presence. "Despite last night's gunplay, he looks well 'nough."

Dobkins shrugs. "Well 'nough ta hang, I s'pose."

~*~

As Snarel walks, the two riders follow along behind him. The tracker is the first to notice someone riding in on their left. "O'r yonder... Rider comin'..." Elkman cradles his rifle in the crook of his arm and turns in his saddle. He cocks the hammer and readies himself for an encounter. Stopping their horses, they watch as the rider lopes closer. Then, from the way he sits a horse, they realize it is McGredy.

The gambler rides up alongside them, not too much worse for wear apart from a bullet scrape across his thigh. McGredy sweeps his hand across his bearded chin and grins. "Glad I found ya both."

Dobkins states simply, "We was ne'er lost."

McGredy looks to the tracker, "Nope, but *I* sure was." He turns his attention to Snarel, who continues to walk on, gaining some distance on them. With a grunt, McGredy casually mentions, "We look t'be about the same as we were a few days ago."

Elkman nods. "Minus a horse..."

As they pick up the pace to catch up with their prisoner, McGredy points a finger. "What're we gonna do with 'im?"

Dobkins is quiet on the matter, but Elkman replies. "We'll go back to the Indians, git Amy and continue on."

Surprised at the answer, McGredy scratches under his chin and wonders aloud. "Hell... Wouldn't we be justified in hangin' 'im now, and then jest be on our way?"

Elkman understands the insinuation. "And *leave* her...?"

"Once we're done with *him*, ya could slip away *real easy*. Ya go back there, and she'll expect ya to act like a *husband*."

Elkman stares forward. "I s'pose she will."

They ride along a while longer, until McGredy notices that they are still traveling in the direction of the Indian village. He glances at Elkman and murmurs, "Want me t'find a tree?"

"Nope..."

"Ya still goin' back t'git her?"

"Yep..."

McGredy shakes his head in disbelief and adjusts his hat. "That's what I like 'bout ya. Yer *stick-to-it*-ness..."

Dobkins looks over at them both, then back to Snarel. When the prisoner turns to look at them, the tracker raises an eyebrow and motions with the end of his gun to keep going. "Jest keep walkin'. We'll let ya know when it concerns ya."

Chapter 45

With Snarel on foot, the group approaches the Indian village. Staring with curiosity at the white party's return, the villagers gather to watch. As they near, the chief steps forward from the crowd with a few words of greeting.

Elkman and McGredy turn to Dobkins for translation. The tracker thinks briefly on the message, then finally conveys, "The chief welcomes us back here. Thankin' us fer bringing the kill'r of the young man..." Taking a moment to find the words, he then adds, "And, they will give punishm'nt."

Elkman turns to McGredy and then speaks to Dobkins. "Tell 'im thanks, but we'll be takin' 'im with us."

Sitting straight in the saddle while addressing the chief, the tracker, with a shake of his head, points at their prisoner. The chief replies with a gesture toward a grieving woman standing with her children. Dobkins nods his understanding and then translates for the others. "Says he kilt her oldest boy. There's no father alive, so the village must avenge his death."

Under his breath, McGredy pipes in. "Fine by me. I bet what they have in store for 'im is *worse* than hangin'."

Pushing through the crowd, Amy steps forward. "No...! He will pay for the murder of my brother and uncle."

When he sees her, Elkman warily weighs their options. Before he has a chance to respond, McGredy states, "Damn... When ya git a woman involved, things do git complicated."

Dobkins listens, as the Indian leader speaks passionately about the need to avenge the fatherless boy. He translates, "They will keep him t'be punished."

As a murmur of contention travels through the crowd, Elkman gets an uneasy feeling and turns to the interpreter. "That was a whole lotta words for jest that."

Dobkins adds, "He also had a few strong suggestions on how ya should control yer woman."

Realizing his situation could get a whole lot worse, Snarel goes to Elkman, looks up defenselessly and pleads, *"Don't leave me with these savages..."*

McGredy snorts, "You've had experience b'fore."

"Quiet... The both of ya." Elkman looks to Dobkins. "Tell the chief that we would like to rest and talk amongst ourselves before decidin' on this man's fate."

The tracker translates Elkman's message for the chief, and they exchange banter that sounds very confrontational. Using hand gestures, they finally to come to agreement. Elkman notices a look of uncertainty on Dobkins' face. "So… What was all that?"

"We are allowed t'stay fer a short while."

"And…?"

"We can watch 'em punish Snarel, if'n we choose."

The horses nervously step back, as several braves move in to take hold of Snarel. The prisoner resists them and looks back at Elkman and McGredy. "Don't leave me to t*hem!"*

The gambler smirks. "Or, what…?"

Glaring at McGredy, Snarel hisses, *"You'll git yers!"*

When Amy moves forward, Elkman lowers an arm down to hold her back. "Let it be. For now…"

She looks up in protest. "He's *ours* to punish!"

He speaks to her in a quiet tone, "Won't do yer deceased kin any good t'get us crosswise with these people."

As tears fill her eyes, she turns to the tracker and begs. "Please… *Tell* them, Dobkins."

"I *already* done told 'em."

Elkman gently restrains Amy, as Snarel, still calling for their help, is dragged away. "Ya all *know* this ain't right…! *Dammit!* Don't let these savages have their way with me!!!"

Amy turns away from Snarel's pleas. Holding firm to Elkman, she cries, *"I wish he was dead already…!"*

Hand on her shoulder, Elkman gives a squeeze. "Soon 'nough… It happens to us *all*, soon 'nough."

Chapter 46

Elkman wakes to see Amy staring at him. He looks around the wickiup, getting his bearings, and then he turns back to her. "How long have ya been watchin' me?"

"You slept a long time."

"I needed it." Peering beyond the entryway, he notices the activity of the villagers. "What's goin' on?"

"You haven't missed anything. Jefferson and Dobkins are around somewhere, and that murderer is under guard."

Elkman sits up, sweeps his hair back and puts on his hat. Looking at the gun in his holster that he recovered from Snarel, he considers leaving it off. "McGredy is prob'ly tryin' ta scare up a game. I better check on them."

She puts a hand on his arm to stop him from standing. "Tomas, wait a moment…"

"What is it?"

"Are we *really* married?"

He meets her gaze, then answers simply. "Yes..."

Unusually quiet, she looks away from him for a second, and then back into his eyes. "It was only an Indian ceremony... Do you consider me your wife?"

Taking a long moment to ponder, Elkman candidly asks, "Do ya *want* me to be yer husband?"

"Yes."

"Okay..." When he starts to get up, she stops him.

"You don't have to stick by it."

"I know..."

She bites her lip and averts her gaze. "It only means something if you *want* it to."

"*Most* marriages are that way."

He starts to stand up again, but she continues to hold him back. "Just wait a minute. I need to talk."

Elkman eases down, gets comfortable and then faces her. "McGredy warned me 'bout this part."

She smiles, looks out the entryway and shakes her head. "What could *he* possibly know?"

"He's known a *few* women."

She turns back to face him and forces her words. "And, I've known a few *men*..." He doesn't respond, so she continues, "I won't hold you to your vows."

"That's okay... I'll hold 'em."

About to cry, she states, "Before we met, I was no angel."

He takes hold of her hands and cradles them in his. "Wasn't 'xpectin' t'find an angel."

"There's a reason my father brought me home to the ranch from out east. Things were different there, and my life... It was a very different life." Sensing that she's got more to get off her chest, he keeps quiet as she continues. "I've had several men court me..."

"That's fine."

"I want to be honest with you." Managing her nerves, she adds, "That's all I have to offer."

"Honesty isn't always the best gift, but I'll take it."

She stares at him, relieved to have aired her doubts, but unsure about his reaction. "You're a different sort of man."

"I guess ya've signed on ta find out."

She smiles sweetly and squeezes her hands around his. "Yes... But, I think I can handle it."

Elkman gets up, grabs his pistol belt, and buckles it on. He stares at her, as he swipes a finger under his moustache. "We'll see..." After grabbing his rifle, he steps outside.

~*~

The late afternoon sun dips low on the horizon, as Elkman searches the village for his friends. He finds McGredy smoking a fat cigar while sitting comfortably outside a lodge. The gambler exhales a smoke ring, while Elkman comments, "Figured I'd find ya in a game of chance somewheres."

McGredy takes the cig from his mouth and tips the ash. "Not sure what they roll into these, but they're mighty tasty." He takes another puff and looks up at Elkman. "I'd have a game goin', if'n there was anyone t'play."

Scanning the village, Elkman notices only a few women and children around. "What's doin'…?"

"They're havin' a pow-wow t'decide our ol' friend's fate."

Elkman glances to the chief's lodge and notices smoke curling up through a hole in the roof. "What do ya think…? Any chance of gittin' 'im back?"

McGredy puffs on the cigar and tilts his head. "They let Dobkins sit in on the proceedings, but I don't figger it likely we'll see Snarel hang fer his crimes."

"She'll be some disappointed."

The gambler sports a grin. "She's a married woman now, so she should git used to it."

With a disapproving glare, Elkman asks, "How many times *you* been married?"

"None…"

"Then, what d'*you* know 'bout it?"

"I ain't n'er bin kicked by a mule, but I figure I wouldn't like it none."

Elkman sets the butt of his rifle on the toe of his boot. "We should light outta here when the decision is made."

"I think it's bin made. We jest ain't acceptin' it yet…"

They glance around at the village, and then Elkman asks, "Where will ya go?"

"I ain't decided. How 'bout *you?*"

Elkman pauses for a moment, thinks, and then answers. "We're headin' to her uncle's place, 'n try to make a go of it." Elkman cracks a smile and offers, "McGredy, yer welcome ta come along."

The gambler blows a puff of smoke and shakes his head. "Sounds like a bunch of work, and ya don't need me intrudin' in yer wedded bliss."

Comfortable with silence, neither speaks for a while. Finally, Elkman looks over to the chief's lodge and murmurs, "She'll be disappointed."

"In marryin' ya…?"

"No… In not gettin' her justice…"

McGredy ashes his cigar and then takes another drag. "Gettin' revenge ain't the nicest way ta start a relationship." The two fall quiet again, and they gaze off to where the last hints of daylight fade behind the mountains.

Chapter 47

A clamor of hoofbeats rouses Elkman from his sleep. In the faint, dawn light, he pulls back the blanket to get up and turns to see Amy curled beside him. He pushes the blanket over the entryway aside to see a group of horsemen gathered outside. Numbering in the twenties, they are all armed for battle. Already at the scene, Dobkins is serving as translator between the riders and the Indian warriors.

Rifle in hand, Elkman strides over to join McGredy, who is only partially dressed. He greets Elkman in a hushed tone. "We weren't gonna disturb ya yet, but things might be serious."

"Who *are* they?"

"Some of 'em are from the boomtown yonder. The others from a burg further west we spent jail-time in."

Elkman studies them and then looks back at McGredy. "A posse…?"

"Or, ya could call 'em a *lynch* mob."

"For *him…?*"

"No… *Us…!*"

Elkman recognizes a few of them, taking note of the sheriff and his deputies. The officer abruptly turns and points. "He's the other one we'll be takin' with us."

McGredy puts up both hands to calm the situation. "Hold it now… Ain't Dobkins explained?"

The sheriff nods his head. "He's said plenty, but I know what we found, and nothin'll change that."

McGredy pleads, "Ya ain't seen the *half* of it."

"Them *dead* men ya left behind say enough."

One of the posse riders from Sawtooth City calls out, "Yer the fellas who shot up our'n."

Considering the turn of events, Elkman looks to Snarel, who stands, hands bound, amongst the Indian braves. That old, familiar grin creeps across the outlaw's bearded features, as his gaze connects with his former trail partner. Elkman looks away, instantly regretting not having put an end to this earlier.

The sheriff nudges his horse forward and points again. "We're takin' y'all back to stand before a judge."

Dobkins positions himself next to Elkman and whispers, "Neither side is gonna let this go without a fight."

After taking a quick headcount of the sheriff's posse, Elkman steps up to speak. "This won't end well for *anyone. These* people want justice for the killin' of one of theirs, and all *we* did was defend our lives."

The sheriff places his hand on the butt of his revolver. "Then, come peaceably, or there'll be others that git hurt."

Elkman clenches his jaw when he notices Amy come outside to see what's going on. Feeling the need to hurry things, he calmly answers, "I'll go with y'all and explain everything, but ya need to let these others alone."

The sheriff looks around and then offers Dobkins a nod. "I've known that negro tracker, and we got no beef with him." Then, pointing at McGredy, he continues, "We want the ones responsible for those that come after ya who are now dead."

Amy struts over and calls out. "I killed them..."

Elkman gives McGredy a shove toward her and hisses, "Keep her quiet, will ya. *I'll* take care of this."

"She's *yer* wife..."

"Jest *do* it..."

Elkman steps closer to the sheriff, looks up at him and offers his rifle. "I'm responsible and will explain it to a judge." Behind him, McGredy intercepts Amy and steers her away.

The sheriff sums up the situation, looks to his men, and then nods his acceptance. "Fine... *You* come with us, he stays, and the others can go spit."

Snarel steps forward and is promptly pulled back again. "Hey, now...! That's *not* how it *goes*. These savages will *murder* me if'n I'm left here. Remember... *I'm* the one who *paid* ya!!!"

The sheriff shakes his head and tucks the rifle on his lap. "Go ahead 'n buy yerself outta this one. I'm *finished* with ya." He looks down at Elkman. "Git yerself a horse, and we'll go."

One of the posse members leans toward the sheriff. "What about his other shooter?"

The sheriff glances at Elkman's gun and replies, "He's comin' along voluntary, so he can hold onto it."

There is a grumble among the riders, and Snarel keenly observes the discontent. Prodding, he blurts out, "He ain't even the one who shot those men. Them *others* are responsible!"

The sheriff waves a dismissing hand and turns away. McGredy leers at Snarel, giving him a smug grin for all the grief he's caused them. In desperation, Snarel reaches over and grabs a knife from one of his captors. He breaks free, plunges the blade into the man and lunges at one of the posse members. Before anyone can stop him, Snarel pulls the rider down and takes his firearm. He swings into the saddle and fires a shot.

Chapter 48

Struck in the chest, McGredy tumbles back. Dobkins steps forward with a shotgun and fires a blast from one of the barrels. As the posse scatters, several of them are peppered with lead.

Surprisingly, Snarel avoids the brunt of the shotgun blast and snaps off another gunshot, this time at a warrior charging toward him. The bullet smacks the man's forehead and drops him dead. The outlaw wheels his horse around, tucks the gun in his lap and attempts to pull his wrists free from the ties that bind them.

The posse scrambles for their weapons while attempting to control their skittish animals. As the melee quickly unfolds, Amy kneels beside McGredy and examines his bullet wound. Elkman snatches his rifle from the sheriff, cocks it, and raises it to aim at Snarel. Just as he squeezes the trigger, one of the posse riders passes in front of him and accidentally takes the bullet. Elkman turns to Amy. "Git *back...*"

"McGredy is wounded!"

They look to Dobkins, just as the tracker lets off the other barrel of the shotgun. A lifeless rider drops from the saddle, and the panicked horse darts into the crowd. Elkman calls, "Dobkins, can ya cover 'em...?"

In spite of the distraction of gunfire, shrieking horses, and people rushing away, Dobkins methodically reloads and steps over to protect Amy and McGredy. Focused on Snarel, Elkman levers a round into his rifle and charges him on foot.

Horseback, the sheriff manages to get between them and directs the aim of his gun at Elkman, stopping him in his tracks. "Hold it... Stop, 'nd throw down yer weapons."

Elkman looks past the lawman to see Snarel wheel his horse around, grin wickedly and point his pistol at the sheriff. Elkman gestures with the barrel of his rifle. *"Behind you...!"*

The sheriff shakes his head and jabs his gun at Elkman. "I'm not that damn naïve..." Just as the words escape his lips, a gunshot tears through his midsection, and the sheriff peers down at the bloody wound. Before dropping from his horse, the lawman has time to turn and see Snarel smile and then blow smoke from his gun.

With his hands still tied, Snarel fires again and hollers, "Hey, Sheriff... I guess it'll be *you* left here t'die instead of *me!*" He shoots at a passing rider, then turns and gallops off.

From the ground, the sheriff looks up. He opens his mouth to speak, but no words come, as he takes his last breath. As several riders rushing past nearly step on the dead man, Elkman grabs the reins of the lawman's horse and slips his boot in the stirrup. The popping of gunfire has the animal in a panic, and the horse spins around in an attempt to flee. Pulling the bridle around to hold the horse's head close to its shoulder, Elkman manages to get a leg over the saddle. Then, he points the excited animal in the direction of Snarel's departure.

The outlaw pauses to fire another gunshot at a fleeing pair of Indians. He laughs to himself, as he tosses the pistol away and pulls a rifle from its scabbard. He levers it and aims, but before he can squeeze off the shot, a warrior rushes him. Snarel is tackled and knocked off his horse. The rifle discharges and tumbles to the ground, as the two land in a tangle of limbs. Snarel is the first to his feet, and he uses his advantage to swing his bound hands at the warrior's head. After the impact of the clenched fists knocks the Indian to the dirt, Snarel picks up the rifle and levers a fresh cartridge. Then, a shot tearing into the ground near his feet gets Snarel's attention. Instead of shooting the prone warrior, Snarel redirects his aim and fires.

At a hard gallop, Elkman levers his Winchester again. He is about to fire, when Snarel's bullet strikes the slab-side of the rifle, knocking it from his grip. Momentarily distracted, Elkman discovers he's not wounded and continues forward.

With Elkman only yards away, Snarel levers his gun, and lifts the rifle to his shoulder. Before the gun goes off, Elkman leaps from the saddle and crashes into him. On the ground, they fight like wildcats. As Snarel uses his clenched fists to smash Elkman and knock him off balance, he declares, "By gawd, we'll finish it *this* time!"

Elkman regains his feet and charges toward Snarel. "*Finally...*"

Chapter 49

As Elkman and Snarel viciously punch and tear at each other, the skirmish in the native village begins to wind down. Haphazardly, the surviving posse members split up and retreat. In Amy's arms, McGredy, wounded, but still conscious, sits up and grips the injury on his chest. "They ain't kilt me yet."

She holds him close to keep him from trying to stand. "How do you feel?"

"Like I got shot…"

As the fighting breaks up, Amy scans the field while stopping Mcgredy's repeated attempts to rise. "How bad is it?"

He watches Dobkins shoot and then reload the shotgun. "It didn't hit my heart."

"I doubt *anyone* could find a target *that* small."

McGredy grimaces, as he turns to give her a sour look. "Hey, now... Save the cruel jabs for yer new husband."

"When he shares advice he got from you about woman, I can't help but redirect my womanly scorn."

Holding back a chuckle, he grins to keep from hurting. "That fella is gonna have his hands full with *you*."

"That is, if he sticks."

"Oh, he's sticker. He ain't got ridda *me* yet."

She smiles. "We'll see what *I* can do about that."

Pain shows on the gambler's face, as he tries again to quell his laughter. "Stop teasin', or it'll move t'bullet 'round."

She turns his torso and sees an exit wound on his back. Tilting her head at him, she says, "Quit all the bellyaching... That bullet passed right through."

"Ya sure I wasn't shot twice?"

"Probably got less than you deserve..." She looks up to see that the major conflict has ended. While warriors strip the losers of their possessions, women and children gather around the dead and tend to the wounded.

At the outskirts of the village, Elkman and Snarel are stumbling their way closer. Elkman holds a gun on the outlaw and pushes him to where the sheriff lies dead on the ground. Seeing Amy cradling McGredy, Elkman asks, "Is he hurt bad?"

"Not too bad..."

"What's he grinnin' 'bout?"

The gambler painfully shifts his position and reaches an arm around Amy. "Sorry pardner, I done stole yer wife."

Snarel spits in his direction. "Damn yer hide, McGredy. Thought I at least done kilt you this time."

With the last of his strength, Elkman swings out and smashes Snarel across the jaw, knocking him to the ground. "I've already heard 'nough of yer mouth..." Recovering slowly, the outlaw sits up but decides to stay put. As the rest of them survey the battle-ravaged village, Elkman looks down at Snarel and spits his words. "This is *yer* doin'..."

The outlaw smirks and rubs his jaw. "You had yerself a hand in it too."

Dobkins snaps the barrel of his reloaded shotgun shut. He walks over and stands directly behind Snarel. "Mista, don't ya worry none 'bout *him* no more." He nudges Snarel with his toe and lowers the aim of the gun. "I's got 'im."

Relieved, Elkman heads over to Amy and McGredy. After stumbling another step, a sudden wave of darkness sweeps over him. He stops, then crumples to the ground, exhausted. With little hesitation, Amy unceremoniously dumps McGredy at her feet. As she cradles Elkman in her arms, the last thing he sees before passing out is her face.

Chapter 50

The native village has recovered from the skirmish. With a bandage wrapped around his middle, McGredy looks ready to hit the gaming tables again. He watches, as Elkman and Amy mount their horses and ride toward him. He meets them, stretches, and asks, "Ya off t'that spread in Montana?"

Elkman tips his hat back, glances at Amy, and replies, "Figured we'd give it a go. How're ya feelin'?"

McGredy touches his unbuttoned vest where a hole has been patched in the fabric. "Put a hole in my fav'rit pocket…"

Noticing the bandage behind the place where McGredy usually deposits his money, Elkman suggests, "Lucky thing the bullet hit ya where ya stow yer funds."

The gambler puts his hand over his heart and grimaces. "Nothin' much t'hide b'hind… We was in a hurry ta leave that boomtown's waterin' hole, so most of it sat on the table."

"Warn't the first time..."

McGredy scratches under his beard and wonders. "Don't s'pose ya wanna go back there with me again?"

Elkman glances at Amy, and then smoothes his moustache from his lip. "Nope..."

"That's okay, pard, Dobkins said he'd t'hang 'round 'n check things out with me."

"Think he can keep ya outta trouble?"

"He can sure *try*."

The tracker stands with his shotgun laid over his arm. "It's bin nice ridin' wit' ya, Mista Elkman." Lifting his hat brim, he lowers his chin. "The missus, as well..."

Amy smiles at him. "You take care of each other."

Dobkins puts his hat back on and nods his appreciation. "And, *you* do the *same*."

As Elkman turns his horse to leave, he hesitates and looks back at McGredy. "Send me a note when this thing with 'im is finally done."

The gambler glances toward one of the wickiups and then back to his partner. "We'll stick 'round 'nd be *sure* it happens *this* time. I'll post ya afterward."

Taking a deep breath, Amy looks around the village. "That Indian boy was not much younger than my brother. There were so many experiences he cheated them both out of. Hiim taking their lives away like that..."

After exchanging a look with McGredy, Elkman tilts his head for Amy to follow. He nudges his horse and then glances back at the gambler once more. "Ya know where ta find me."

McGredy grimaces and gingerly lifts a hand to wave. "Ya bet I do... With the shackles o' marriage holdin' ya down, ya won't git too far, I 'xpect."

Giving the gambler a stern look and the wag of a finger, Amy follows after Elkman. "Don't you go wearing out your welcome even before you come visit."

As they depart, Dobkins steps up next to McGredy and lowly murmurs, "Surprisin' t'me that she don't stay ta witness what's gonna happen to that outlaw."

McGredy gazes after the couple riding off to the east. "Watchin' a man die don't wash away the taste of revenge. Only leavin' it behind can do that."

~*~

The village long behind them, Elkman and Amy ride with only the clothes on their backs and what they can carry on their saddles. With thoughts of an uncertain future, they stare silently ahead. Amy finally looks over at Elkman. Gratefully, she murmurs, "Thank you for escorting me back to Montana."

"Said I would. Aim t'keep my end of the bargain."

As they ride on, she gazes behind one last time, and then looks to the path ahead. "Yes... That will fulfill your obligation. As far as I'm concerned, you don't have to stay on."

"We'll see how everythin' strikes ya when we git there. Ne'er know how a person might feel 'bout somethin' 'til they're in the midst of it."

Wishing to change the subject, she clenches her jaw and looks around. "I would sure like to see that evil man get what he has coming to him."

Elkman glances over and remarks, "We all git what's comin' in the end. Bearin' witness to it don't make the feelin's go away."

"Well… Uh… Thank you."

"What for?"

After a moment, she turns to look straight at him. "I thank you for not leaving me back there in that Indian village to be married to someone not of my choosing."

"Am *I* of yer choosin'?"

"Mostly…"

Elkman swipes a finger under his moustache. "Told me I could bring ya back, if ya don't please me."

Her jaw drops. "And, what did *you* tell *them?*"

"Poss'bly, I'd trade ya for a good horse."

With a performative air of insult, she asks in a huff, "Mister Elkman, is that all I'm worth to you?"

With a wry smile, Elkman replies, "Well, the thing is… A good horse'll be kept for life 'n, despite the occasional bucks, ya only remember the good times."

She taps her heels to hurry her mount. "Husband, I *do* suppose we may have a few bucks along the way."

Elkman nods, as he brings his horse to a trot to catch up to her. "I wouldn't have it any other way."

She reaches out a hand to touch his, and he gives hers a tender squeeze before releasing it. Thoughts of the outlaw and native village fade away, as they urge their horses into a lope toward new horizons in Montana.

The End…

If you enjoyed ***Elkman & McGredy***,
read other stories by

Eric H. Heisner

www.leandogproductions.com

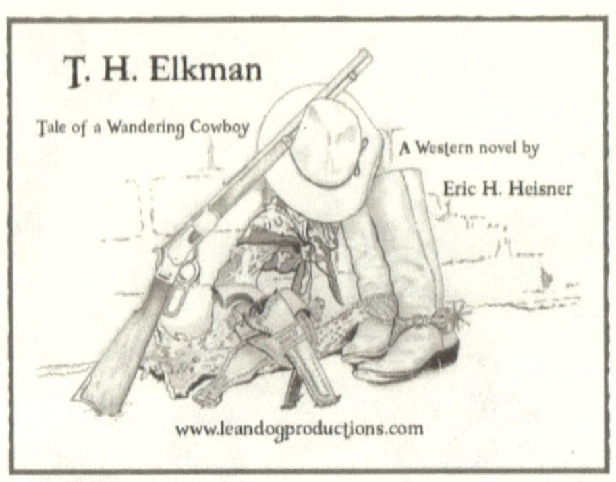
T. H. Elkman
Tale of a Wandering Cowboy
A Western novel by
Eric H. Heisner
www.leandogproductions.com

WEST TO BRAVO
A Western Novel
By Eric H. Heisner
WWW.LEANDOGPRODUCTIONS.COM

Wings of the Pirate
A high-flying Adventure Novel
By Eric H. Heisner
Limited time pre-order at:
www.inkshares.com
illustrations by
Al P. Bringas
www.leandogproductions.com

Eric H. Heisner is an award-winning writer, actor, and filmmaker. He is the author of several Western and Adventure novels: *West to Bravo, T. H. Elkman, Africa Tusk, Conch Republic,* and *Short Western Tales: Friend of the Devil*. He can be contacted at his website:
www.leandogproductions.com

Al P. Bringas is a cowboy artist, actor, and horse lover. He had done illustrations for novels including, *T. H. Elkman*, the *West to Bravo* series, *Wings of the Pirate* and *Mexico Sky*. He lives and works in Southern California.

www.ingramcontent.com/pod-product-compliance
Lightning Source LLC
LaVergne TN
LVHW091049080826
845145LV00002B/681